Bridal Brunch

NORMA L. JARRETT

ISBN-13: 978-1499391930
ISBN-10: 1499391935

DEDICATION

To God for this gift, to my parents, Norman and Ethel Jarrett for giving me earthly life, love and support and to all the "Brunch Ladies" of the world–*Jeremiah 1:5*.

Praise for Norma L. Jarrett Books

Sunday Brunch

"How fun and how rare is this that once in a famished while, sistas are able to gorge on the delicious morsels of such a literary cuisine...Enjoy!" *–Vivica A. Fox, Actress*

"

"Readers craving juicy plotlines driven by decent and compelling characters will always find a kindred spirit in Jarrett." *–Essence Magazine*

"*Sunday Brunch* portrays and examines 'real life issues' through vivid and relatable characters." *–Victoria Christopher Murray, bestselling author*

"...These women are my friends, my associates... my environment." *–Charnele Brown, Actress*

Sweet Magnolia

"Like family conversations at the table, the author delivers real issues from characters larger than life." *–Upscale Magazine*

"... (a) Sweet inspirational offering..." *–Publisher's Weekly*

"...appealing characters that resonate in our soul."
–Jacquelin Thomas, *bestselling author*

"Norma Jarrett has crafted a beautifully written, soul-stirring story that touches the heart..."
–ReShonda Tate Billingsley, *bestselling author*

"A memorable narrative of redemption and reconciliation..."
–Essence **Magazine**

"Family characters galore fill the inspiring 'Sweet Magnolia'."
–The Times-Picayune

Other books by Norma L. Jarrett

Sunday Brunch
Sunday Brunch Diaries (Essence bestseller)
Sweet Magnolia (Essence Magazine National Book Club Selection)
Brunchspiration: A Quotable Devotional
Christmas Beau (ebook)
Love on a Budget

Coming Soon:
Vineyard Surrender
D.C. Brunch
Brunch at Tiffany's

ACKNOWLEDGMENTS

To God, and I say this respectfully…You rock and I love You ☺. Thanks to my husband Clarence York, brother Stephen Jarrett, sister Paulette Jones and Mary Upshaw (spiritual mom). My Aunt Queenie Ewing for her patience, listening ear and sage advice. That VW Beetle is coming – smile. Thanks to the rest of the Jarrett, Jones, Page and York families; Brunch Ladies worldwide, Lakewood Church (Pastor Joel, Pastor John Gray), Bishop T.D. Jakes, Joyce Meyer and others that feed my soul, my always supportive Sorors of Alpha Kappa Alpha Sorority, Inc., Neptune (original hometown), Houston, North Carolina A & T (Aggie Pride) and Thurgood Marshall School of law family; to all the faithful book fans that show endless love to all authors and anyone else that has shown life and/or literary love and support! Too many to mention but: Denise Williams, Stefani Farris, Tika Hampton (and family – smile), Quinella Minix-Williams, Michele Austin, Audra Foree (representing the line and Alpha Phi – Who's the Boss?); Wanda Mathews, Alzaada Manns, Jetola Anderson-Blair, Eva G. Headley (Natasha Smith – smile), Janet Hill-Talbert, Essence Magazine, Patrik Henry Bass, Girlfriends Pray (that prayer line!) Tracy Hines-Winston, "Super Fan" LaToya Williams…hate shout outs because you always leave someone out! (catchall – charge to my head…not my heart) and to the music makers that feed me on the regular Stephanie Hogan, Mandisa, Mary Mary, Lecrae, Israel Houghton and New Breed, and many others you have no idea *xoxo* Norma

Prologue

Dear Jesus:

I don't have much time, but need to connect. *I know I know…*I'm working on the time management thing. Seems like gone are the days you and I'd hang out for hours, I so miss that. But I know when I've been neglecting my God time. Experience has taught me I can't do *a thing* without You. *Been there, done that…bought the t-shirt.* Since so much is competing for my attention these days: family, work, Facebook, Twitter, Instagram (seriously), I need to work a little harder. And I'm enlisting Your help!

Hubby Chris has been working second shift at the police department, keeping the streets of Houston safe. Please keep him covered. Right now, he's sound asleep, calling *major* hogs. *Side note: You could've given me the heads up about that.* Little Chris has gotten out his bed and tucked his narrow self under his dad. It's the cutest thing ever. There're times when I wish I could freeze this moment. It's just that good. You know, that season after all the rain, struggle, doubt, and heartache dissipate. They take their funky remnants and bounce! The dust settles. The harvest not only arrives, it's abundant! Ahhhh, nothing like beauty for ashes!

I've struggled for so long to be the woman You designed me to be. And I *finally* get it! I don't have to be perfect. I just need to be consistent in my faith and trust the process. *Phew!* I could have saved myself years of anxiety, fear, and emotional breakdowns. You've been in total control but I insisted on grabbing that steering wheel. Driving us both nuts! Thank You for being such a patient and loving God.

I always knew there was this confident woman inside of me. But You allowed the world to see it. I knew I was destined to be a wife and mother. I knew I was something greater than just everyone else's confidante, friend, problem fixer or prayer partner. Don't get me wrong. I truly love helping others, especially my girls–Jewel, with all her crazy, unpredictable over the top ways; Capri, my solid as a rock law partner; Angel, my mature, smart and savvy mentor; and Jermane, my classy, sweet friend who refuses to let me pay back that loan from law school. These are my ride-or-die (can you say that over thirty?) sister-friends. Through thick and thin, broken hearts, marriage, law school, business start-ups, career shifts, childbirth, and holidays; we've fought, argued, cried, worshiped and celebrated...together.

Guess we have Jewel, the woman who can throw confetti in the midst of any crisis, to thank for our first "bonding" brunch back in law school. I thought it was a little over the top, because honestly who could afford Sunday Brunch back in law school? But that's my beloved Jewel. Just like her name, she brings the sparkle and shine every time.

My gratitude reflection for this season starts with my family—my awesome and anointed husband Chris and our son, his moniker and mini-me. I'm grateful for the good, the great, the "what in the world" and the "shut the front door" moments. I'm also grateful for the lessons. I've clearly learned that life is dynamic. I've learned to be comfortable with being uncomfortable.

Do I like it? No. My flesh HATES it. But I know if I stay with You I can ride anything out, bloom where I'm planted, and come out on top! This morning, I didn't spend long in the Bible. I started in Proverbs. If all else fails, Proverbs has an answer. It's saturated with wisdom. It's my fail safe – smile. Then my daily devotional led me to John 15:30…

Greater love has no one than this that someone lay down his life for his friends.

I closed my Bible right then, assured I'd gotten my word for the day. I'm grateful this morning for *my* friends. We've "laid down our lives" for each other many a time. Maybe not literally, but we have each other's backs. We take care of each other. We're more than friends…we're like a small gang, lol. And I'm proud of us. I'm proud of what we've accomplished, how we carry ourselves and the way we love. We know our worth. We're leaders, business owners, wives, mothers, givers and hard workers. But even more precious than that, we are forever…

"Brunch Ladies"

xoxo…

Lexi

Chapter 1 - Beautiful Ordinary Life

Jewel threw an arm across her husband Kevin's waist and buried her nose in the small of his back. A few moments later, she hurled her body in the opposite direction, instantly barricaded by a dog and a slobbering kid. *This is ridiculous.* She rolled on her back and stared at the ceiling fan. *How did we get here, God?* She finally eased out the cover and climbed over her husband. As soon as one foot hit the floor she felt something wet. "Ugh! Tinka!" In seconds, her Shih Tzu had dived off the bed and commenced to devouring her foot.

"C'mon babe whatchu doing?" Her husband grumbled and shifted beneath the cover.

Jewel rolled her eyes and took a few steps to the master bathroom. She dropped onto the toilet seat. *This seat is cold; Kevin must have turned on that air again.* Her head rolled back, as items scrolled through her mind like movie credits. In seconds, Tinka burst through the bathroom door. *Can't I have any peace?*

"I don't bother you when you have to go," she scolded.

Tinka barked as her big brown eyes locked with Jewel's. She sighed and put her head down. When Jewel finished, she walked over to the sink, splashed water on her face, and walked out the bathroom.

"Babe, you seen my blue and red tie?" Kevin yelled from the closet the moment she stepped into the bedroom. "I never had this problem when I was wearing that parcel delivery uniform, ah the perks of a Commodity Supervisor!"

Uh, yeah whatever. Jewel closed her eyes tight, took a deep breath, and then opened them. "On your tie rack behind the blue and green one."

"Shoot, I'm running behind! Why didn't you wake me up sooner?" He snatched a pair of slacks from the closet and threw them on the bed.

Translation: Can you make me a cup of coffee and find my socks? Jewel grabbed his socks and put them atop the dresser.

"Having lunch with the new Division Manager. He could be the key to my *next* promotion." He pulled out his shoe shine kit. *I knew I should've done this last night.* He set the kit back in the closet.

"Great honey. Great." *At least somebody's making some money.* She had to admit her Fabulous Jewel's Events with Events that Sparkle like Diamonds, was currently having a lackluster moment ...well year. She was more than grateful her husband nabbed a promotion after his leadership training. Suddenly, he was the major breadwinner with benefits.

"Oh, babe, can you iron my favorite boxers?" Kevin said as he turned on the shower.

Really? "Not before I go downstairs and make some coffee." Jewel walked over to the other side of the bed and pulled on her daughter's arm. Her body went limp like a rag doll then showed some signs of life. "Aja baby get up. You have to start sleeping in your own bed. Even your four-year-old brother sleeps in his." Finally, her daughter slid off the bed and rubbed her eyes. "I'm tired," she croaked then yawned.

"Of course you're tired. You brought it on yourself when you and your Daddy decided to sit up and watch TV." Jewel placed her hands on both her shoulders and guided her daughter out the door. "Now you got the Monday morning blues," she barked as they schlepped down the hall.

Chapter 2 – Mompreneur

After getting her husband and daughter out the door and her son to kindergarten, Jewel needed a reboot. She juiced some fruit and veggies then sat at her desk. Dressed in her comfy yoga pants and t-shirt, she flipped on her computer and exhaled. Her appointment calendar popped up. *Who am I kidding—no seeds, no harvest = no income.* She crossed her arms and leaned back. *God, it's official, I'm in a slump.*

Her fingers typed the address to her favorite fashion blog. *Sure wish I knew how to sew.* Then she spent twenty minutes scrolling through Pinterest. *Just forget it.* She pushed away from her desk and moved to the couch, where she pondered her decision to abandon her law career to pursue her passion. *That's what I get for watching too much Oprah. Follow your passion…live your best life, good for you "O".* After Kelly and Michael, where she spent time wondering why Michael wouldn't close his gap, *The View* and a few reruns of *I Love Lucy,* she grabbed her phone. "Lexi," she barked. Her phone dialed. In seconds her bestie answered.

"Jewel, don't you have a fabulous soiree to plan or some future clients to suck up to?" Lexi slid the door to her file cabinet shut then rolled her chair back to her desk.

"And are *we* violating one of Jewel's phone rules?" She sang, "One does not put one on speaker without acquiring permission first…"

Lexi rolled her eyes. "Jewel, what's so urgent that you had to call me early on a Monday morning?"

"Well, I don't want to be one of those whiny complaining sisters…"

Since when?

"But, I Jewel Antoinette Whitaker-Eastland, events planner extraordinaire am officially… in a slump." Her shoulders dropped as she exhaled.

"Jewel, sweetie, you know this comes with the territory. Got to roll with the tide. I warned you." Lexi scrolled through her e-mails. *Oh no he didn't! He's got me confused. I'm not afraid to go to trial.* Her fingers rapidly pecked a response.

"I just don't get it." Jewel walked over to her desk and dropped into her chair. "When I first launched, I was the hottest events planner in H-town! I had to turn away business. Everyone who was anyone wanted my services. Can you blame them? I am Fabulous Jewels, the original fairy glam mother, the go-to glitter goddess…the platinum planner." Her eyes skimmed her Facebook timeline.

"Jewel, no one's exempt from a dry spell." Lexi kept her eyes on her computer as she continued to scroll. *What? Oh, they want to set up a deposition? Bring it…*

"My point, if you were listening, is, I've hit a wall … and despite all my tried and true methods it won't budge. For the life of me I can't understand why God would give me this grand vision and leave me to wander in a desert?" Jewel's fingertips paused on her keys, "Omigod? Could I be headed for an Israelite experience? Surely God knows I don't have the wherewithal for that! I mean how many seasons of sacrifice, trials by fire, and business baptism does a girl need?" Jewel clicked on her Twitter page and retweeted from Idris Elba, Tyler Perry, David Tutera, Joel Osteen and Kevin Hart.

Lexi placed both her hands over her face and rubbed her forehead with her fingertips. *Why me God?* "Jewel, I don't think He'd do that. But if so, it's for a reason." She scrolled through her e-mails and hit print. "Have you brainstormed to find some new ideas to get some momentum? How about a little rebranding, run an ad, or here's a stretch...stay off Facebook and Twitter!" She slid over and grabbed a document off the printer.

"I beg your pardon; you've never gotten a Candy Crush game request from *Moi.* All I wanted was a little empathy. Here I was thinking we could find a little common ground, one 'shepreneur' to another." If I wanted to be chastised I would have called Capri, your law partner. I mean it's not like Reynold's and Stanton has always been balling out of control. When you guys hit those rough spots, I was here for you!"

Oh brother. "Jewel, I've been supportive. And FYI, if you were anyone else I would have hung up a long time ago, so don't push it. I think this is just a little reality check. No one said it'd be all glitter and glam. But if anybody can do this, *you* can. I remember the first day I met you during the first week of law school." Lexi smiled and leaned back in her chair. "This is the *same* Jewel that stormed Financial Aid that day and got both our checks! In the words of Mandisa, *You were born for this!*"

"Who?" Jewel quickly Googled her name.

"She's this gospel artist…never mind. Jewel, if what you're doing isn't working, get creative. Swallow your pride a little and come out your comfort zone. Join a few organizations. You love people and they love you, well not everyone, but you get the point." Lexi put on her glasses and flipped several pages of a contract. "In other words, the clients are not gonna just show up at Westminster Oaks."

Jewel rolled her eyes. "I don't know, Lex, gosh ...who has time for that? I mean I have a husband and two kids." She grabbed a nail file from her pencil cup and ran it across her tips.

"Uh, I have a husband and a kid, but I make time to get involved in the things that add value to my business. And you know I'm not a people person, I've learned to adjust. It's how we grow."

"I forgot Lexi's superwoman all of a sudden." She mocked, sucked her teeth and grabbed her bottle of clear polish.

"Jewel, I'm done. You called *me* for advice remember? So I'm telling you what's worked for me. When I have to 'move some mountains' I get up extra early, study the word, speak affirmations and talk to God until He talks back! Then I act."

Yeah-yeah, blah, blah. "Girl puleeaze, spare me with the rah-rah Joel Osteen routine. I've talked to God until I was blue in the face. I've been standing in front of my mirror articulating the most eloquently crafted declaration: I, Jewel Antoinette Whitaker-Eastland, Events Planner Extraordinaire am the go-to coordinator for A-list clientele with unlimited budgets. I plan bi-coastal multi-million dollar events that net annual million dollar revenue for my household. Isn't it fabulous? I've been confessing for six months and nothing, nada, nil, dry bones! God just doesn't like me anymore. Maybe you need to come anoint my computer or something," she barked.

"Uh, Jewel, no. I'm not doing that. Besides, you can anoint your own computer. You just need a little patience, God hasn't forgotten about you."

Jewel slapped her palms on the desk. "I hate that word 'patience' ugh!" She noticed a friend request pop up on her

Facebook page. *McKenzie Myers. Myers, Myers, why does that name sound familiar?* There was a generic profile photo of the ocean. *Hmmm.*

"Look Jewel, I love you girl, but I really have to go. Got a meeting in fifteen minutes." *I've wasted enough time with you.*

"Right," she uttered, now distracted. "Oh, don't forget I'm planning an Oscar party at Capri and Anthony's house. But she doesn't know yet. Girls night, please RSVP to the e-invite."

Okay, so when are the Oscars and I'm almost sure it has been deleted from my junk mail. "Sure Jewel, wouldn't miss it. Okay sweetie, seriously gotta go."

Jewel quickly blew on her nails. "Sunday, March 2nd, cause I know you haven't opened the evite. Oh, and you tell that law partner of yours that she can't just go canceling brunch all willy-nilly. Need I remind her? Brunch *is* a privilege, not a right."

Chapter 3 – Friending

After Jewel accepted the friend request from McKenzie Myers, she still didn't gather much more about her. *Doesn't post much. Lots of articles on finance.* Jewel's eyebrow arched. *From LA...engaged.* She did notice her friends appeared to be the who's who of the entertainment and sports industry. *Hmmm.* She jumped up and grabbed some yogurt from the fridge and was headed back to her desk when her phone rang. *Area code 310? I don't know anyone in that area. Could be an old bill collector.* She let it go to voicemail. She went back to surfing on the net and her curiosity got the best of her. She pressed the button and listened to her voicemail.

Jewel Whitaker??? Big sister "Oh-so-fine-and-fabulous-Jewel!" this is Myra Myers. But now it's McKenzie! Will explain when you call back...

Jewel immediately hit the missed phone number to redial. "Yes, can I speak with Myra, I mean McKenzie?"

"Is this THE fabulous Jewel Whitaker? My big sis, mentor, and Soror?"

"Myra? Wow, this is, this is a wonderful surprise? How'd you get my phone number?"

"I have my ways. Actually, the sorority grapevine. Anyways, fantastic news, I'm engaged!" she said with a jubilant shriek. "And when I heard you were an events planner, I had to find you. No one else would do!"

Omigod. "Wow, I'm honored. It's been like forever. Haven't seen you since undergrad."

"Like, I know! So much has changed. So much has happened. But I'll have to tell you more later. I live in L.A. and I'm having the wedding here in six months. Think you can pull it off?"

"Well, I don't know. That's pretty short notice. What kind of budget are you working with? Flying back and forth to L.A. won't come cheap. You know me." She crossed her fingers.

"The budget? Well, Jewel dear…money's no object! And of course, I'll cover the travel…"

"First Class?" Jewel blurted before she knew it.

"Need you even ask? What other way is there to travel?" Her voice buoyant.

Ding, Ding, Ding! Jackpot! Jewel put her fist in the air and pulled it down like the arm of a slot machine. "Oh yes, I believe I can shift some things to accommodate your event. So tell me about your groomy, anyone I know? Do you have a venue or have you picked your colors yet?" *Now I can take you seriously!*

"Well, I'm like 90% certain the venue is the Beverly Hills Hotel, colors I'm not sure but there will be pink!"

"Right…got it." Jewel tried to contain the fireworks and confetti toss happening on the inside. She was already counting her money.

"Jewel, sweetie I have to run. I'm late for a meeting but we'll talk soon, I promise! Toodles."

"Toodles." *Darn, she never told me the name of the groom. Oh well, who cares! Jewel* ran to her computer, clicked on her Spotify Anthem playlist and raised her hands in the air. "This is it God! The big one!" She did the Running Man, Dougie, Wobble and any other dance that came to mind. Then she stopped all of a sudden and looked up and shouted, "Won't He do it!" She ran over to her bulletin board and stared at her affirmation. "Yes He will…God, You did that! I'm sorry for all the times I got mad at You! You still love me!" She paused in the middle of her praise, "This is a great cause for a 911 Brunch! I have the perfect spot, Caracol! I've been looking for a reason to try their brunch! Can't wait til Sunday!" She started dancing again. "Fabulous Jewels is back!"

Chapter 4 – Sunday Morning Live

Capri pressed her thigh against Anthony's as he rubbed her hand. Although she wasn't much of a jewelry person, she still loved the way her custom solitaire glistened under the church lights. The few pieces of jewelry she owned were gifts from her husband. For Capri, their true treasures, each other's hearts, dwelled inside. What they had was real and authentic. In an era of Basketball, Football and whatever other kind of 'Wives', she was more inclined to guard their privacy. Her experience was so foreign to what she'd seen on TV, it grieved her spirit.

Anthony raised her hand and kissed the back of it, instantly prompting her eyes to lock with his during worship. Her insides warmed. *Oooh, I can't have these feelings in church.* "But he *is* my husband," Capri mused. When Anthony joined Living Truth Ministries, her church during and after law school that sealed their union. He had such a willing spirit. Pastor Graves conducted their premarital counseling, which would have been perfect, had Jewel and Kevin, not argued throughout the class. She snapped from her thoughts as Anthony tugged her arm. She clumsily stood, while he slid his hand around her waist.

"Now I normally don't make a fuss about famous folk because everyone is a star in the eyes of the Lord," the short middle-aged man said as he looked over his wire frame glasses. "But you know I'm a diehard Houston Meteors fan." Pastor Graves' chest puffed with pride in the pulpit. So I don't think Jesus would mind if I give a special shout to one of Houston's finest in the NBA Anthony Stanton and his beautiful wife Capri. He looked up, "And Lord I just want to especially thank you for using him in that last minute three point shot to get us in the playoffs." The congregation laughed.

Anthony, always humble, nodded, smiled, and quickly sat down. Capri noticed several women swoon as the couple sat back down. She knew the affect her husband had on women, but there wasn't an ounce of insecurity in her body. As the music cued for the "greet your neighbor" song, everyone rushed over to shake Anthony's hand. That always made Capri uncomfortable.

"This is worship service, not a fan club," she thought. As women and men paraded by, she could not help but wonder whether some of them were dressed for church or a club. *Why does everyone want to look like a celebrity? Caked on make-up, tight dresses, twenty-inch weaves, and logo purses. Lord please help me not to judge.*

~~~~~

"Pastor Graves was on it today!" Lexi said to Capri. "Hold still little Chris," she warned. As her son wrestled, she kept a tight grip on his hands.

"Little Chris, come give your Auntie Capri a kiss." Capri knelt down and he turned away. "I'm gonna steal one anyway," she said as she grabbed his golden chubby cheek.

He wiped it right off in an exaggerated motion.

"Chris! You know better than that," Lexi scolded. "One day you're gonna want a kiss from a pretty lady."

Her son ignored her. "Mommy it's hot, I wanna go home." He whined as he held on to the coloring projects from his Sunday school class, fidgeted and jumped in place.

"Shush Chris, Mommy's talking," she chastised, irritated each time his shoes hit the concrete.

Despite Lexi's annoyance, Capri thought Chris was adorable in his button-down shirt, slacks, suspenders, and newsboy cap. He melted her heart and put a smile on her face.

"Girl, what are you cheesing at?" Lexi quizzed, still struggling to hold her son's hand.

"I don't know, just watching you and little Chris. To think a little over four years ago he wasn't even here. It's just amazing. You're so blessed, Lexi. You got exactly what you prayed for. You wanted it all, now you have it."

"Girl, having it all is overrated! She laughed. "Just kidding." *Sort of.*

It's a lot of work, but I'm happy. With a child, you never have downtime, and I worry about big Chris a lot. He's about to work himself crazy."

"Houston's finest. Better whip that Psalms 91 out daily. Remember Pastor Grave's sermon. He's a protector." Capri glanced at her large watch. "Darn, I have so much work to do."

Lexi waved her finger. "Uh-uh sister, you can't get out of brunch. C'mon girl we need a little break. It's been a minute. Even Angel's coming," she said excitedly.

"Really? Since she joined Lakewood and started advocacy work, we've rarely seen her." Capri noticed that Anthony had just broken from a conversation and was headed their way, but knew, after several people stopping him, he'd be another few minutes. *People can't even let the man worship. He's a basketball player, not God. Sheesh.*

"Nobody told you to marry a baller," Lexi said, as if to read Capri's mind.

"Be quiet girl, I didn't choose him. He *chose* me." She sneered.

"Hmm, I don't think my legal rock star friend would've risked a major career at a huge law firm if she didn't feel the same. So save it." Lexi playfully punched Capri in the arm.

"Whatever." Capri rolled her eyes as she clutched her Bible.

"Whatever what?" Anthony said as he reached his long arms around his wife from behind. He placed his face against hers and kissed her on the cheek. "Hey Lexi. Little man!" He released Capri from his arms, then reached down and scooped up little Chris.

The little boy started giggling and burst into a huge smile. Anthony lowered him to the ground. "That's my man right there." Anthony pulled out his wallet and gave Chris a twenty-dollar bill.

Little Chris's eyes grew large at the sight of the money. He held the bill between his hands and stared at it. "Look mommy I'm rich!"

"Uh sweetie, we need to talk about what it really means to be rich. Put it in your pocket." Lexi placed her hand on her hip and shook her head. "Anthony, you gotta stop doing that. You're always spoiling him."

"You know I'm gonna ignore you. I don't have any of my own to spoil, so why not?"

Capri kept smiling, but something inside stirred at the sound of those words.

"So, where's that knuckle head husband of yours? Tell him I got some tickets if he can ever make it to the game." Anthony playfully punched little Chris as sweat beads formed on his bald head from the sun. He made the little boy stand in front of his legs. "Keep still."

"You know where he is…work. He's got mouths to feed!" Lexi joked.

"Well, we're gonna have to get that brother a 9 to 5 cause' he can't miss worship."

"Now you know Chris isn't gonna miss church. If he has to work a Sunday, he hits up the Saturday night service or even worships with the youth."

"Chris is a good brother," Anthony said.

"Okay, I need to run and drop little Chris off at a birthday party. Capri, see you in a few?"

"Yeah," she sighed, "I'll be there."

Chapter 5 – Mission Statement

Angel sat in the back of the Lakewood youth service and stared at the media screen. Her eyes were glued to every visual. The slide show captured the true spirit of the young adult mission trip to Mexico. She had never imaged when she and Octavio joined Lakewood, that he'd find his true calling so soon. As she watched him excitedly narrate the various slides, his hands danced in the air, and his voice burst with enthusiasm.

Tears formed in her eyes as she saw how he and the young peopled ministered through song, fellowship, food and clothing donations. She watched the teens on stage continuously thank Octavio for his leadership and guidance. She beamed. The worship service came to a close. Octavio made eye contact with Angel while he was talking to a group of people. Shortly after, he climbed down from the stage and walked toward her. She got out of her seat and met him halfway up the aisle.

"Hey you!" Angel hugged Octavio, basking in the familiar warmth of his touch. She closed her eyes taking in his embrace then caught herself.

" So, what'd you think?" He said as he pulled away. His eyes lit up like a little kid showing his class project to his parents.

"It was just anointed! I felt the spirit of the people. I know they were blessed." She smiled. "I'm so proud of you and your team. I see the way those kids look up to you."

Octavio smiled back and their eyes held a momentary gaze. He was about to grab and hold her hand out of habit, but resisted. He ran his hand down the back of his slick dark hair instead. "Wow, you're all vibrant today! That's more than a God glow. What's up?" He eyed her brightly colored outfit.

"What else? Brunch with the girls," she shared.

"Well, yellow suits you. And I like the hair." He winked.

"Still keeping it natural but letting it grow." She tried not to look too long at his olive skin, supple lips and infectious smile. They both paused, trying to figure out how to fill the empty space with something other than their usual conversation.

"You want to come over and meet the rest of the mission

team?" he finally asked with a bit of hope.

"Um, no … better get on my way…" She shrugged one shoulder. "Just wanted to come and support you. I know how hard you worked to make it happen." She held the handles to her purse tight in her hands.

"Right." He stepped back a little. "I need to do some more debriefing with the team. We're already working on the next mission trip." He kept his eyes on her.

"Already? Where?"

"We're partnering with another church. Not quite sure, but I believe Africa or Brazil."

"Oooh, Brazil, definitely want to be prayed up for that!" Angel laughed. "So awesome." She paused not wanting to look away, "Well," She sighed, "gotta go. You know how Jewel is about being late. And well," she shrugged. "I haven't really told everybody."

He took a deep breath. "Okay, glad you came."

"Me too."

Chapter 6 – The Girls Are Back

"Okay, Jewel you know the 911 Brunch is code for emergency. We're only supposed to use it for truly urgent circumstances." Capri pulled out the white chair from the gray wood table and sat down.

Jewel raised her church finger while batting her eyes. "First, may I acknowledge that you're on probation from the last brunch no-show. And may I add that spice color sheath is simply radiant against your copper skin. And are those cinnamon highlights in that fiercely layered bob? I never thought you'd let that boring hair go—Ms. Fierce is for-giv-en!"

"Hi Jermane." Capri ignored Jewel as she eyed the brunch buffet in the distance. "Love this décor."

"Hmpf." Jewel's nose turned upward. "Some people just don't know how to receive forgiveness *or* a compliment. I was going to add that 'spice' is the new black. But nevermind," she uttered in a spasm of irritation.

"Really? Had no idea, it amazes me that people spend time coming up with ten ways to say orange. I just think there are more important things in the world. So what's up? Somebody sick, lost a job, or let me guess. You need a loan *again*?"

Jewel's eyes enlarged. "Do you have to put all my business out there? I thought when you loan people money you aren't supposed to talk about it. It's somewhere in the Bible," Jewel said through clenched teeth as she looked around. "And FYI – I've been making my payments, on time!"

Capri rolled her eyes and nodded toward the door. "There's Angel and Lexi."

Jewel's neck stretched as she peered in that direction. She threw up her hand and the hostess led the women toward their table. "Finally." She eyed her watch.

"Hey ladies, apologies. An accident on the freeway. On top of that, little Chris was so clingy after church. He usually likes to hang with his dad." Lexi pulled out the chair next to Jewel and sat down.

"I would fuss if you weren't looking so cute. That electric blue peplum is so on trend and that white pencil skirt, A-OK after

Labor Day." She winked, "Is fitted to perfection …Loving the tapered hairdo!" Jewel's eyes paused at her feet. "Oh my, I can spot a shoe upgrade a mile away! You can tell when a sister starts making a little extra change."

"Thanks Jewel. Glad you approve. But my bold gold chain and clutch…Forever 21. You know I did "high-low" before it was legit." Lexi's hand ran over her necklace. She fingered her short layers.

Jewel put her hand on the side of her face and turned her head. "Don't they have the *best* accessories?" she said, lowering her voice.

Angel eased into her chair. "I've heard great things about Caracoral's. Can't wait to try the brunch." Beautiful space, her eyes took in a blue and white rug that covered most of the floor, and the halo chandeliers.

"Soo, before we eat, I must brief us on the event that served as the catalyst for the 911brunch," Jewel announced.

"Can't it wait? I'm starved," Capri uttered, deflated.

Jewel grimaced. "As I was saying, I realize the 911 brunch is reserved for emergencies of sorts and major announcements. So here it goes…" She cleared her throat, stood, and smoothed out her chevron print fit and flare dress. "There comes a time in a person's career when something monumental occurs. A defining moment no less, a feather in one's cap, a 'next level' blessing…a door that leads to the unimaginable, unthinkable…"

"Jewel, if you don't get to the point you're going to be sitting here all by your monumental self," Lexi warned.

"Okay, alright. First, giving honor to God, who is my Lord and savior Jesus Christ…" She put her hand on her chest, "I'd like to thank my faithful friend and prayer partner Lexi for being a true source of encouragement—." *Cue the loving gaze.* She turned toward Lexi and smiled affectionately.

Capri put her napkin on the table and started to get up.

"Okay, *okay,* a little patience please," Jewel uttered through clenched teeth. "So, I'd been confessing this affirmation for like six months. And boom! I, Jewel Antoinette Whitaker-Eastland, owner of 'Fabulous Jewels Events with Events that Sparkle like Diamonds' got a breakthrough. Yes, yes, Jesus loves me. I finally heard those words that every events planner wants to hear—Money. Is. No. Object!" She squealed, "Can you believe it? I have my first client with an *unlimited* budget! Fabulous Jewels Events is bicoastal! Sparkle, sparkle shine!" She softly clapped her hands together.

They all looked at one another.

"Great, congratulations. I'm starved, anyone with me?" Angel said as she stood up.

"That's it? *Unbelievable*. Don't y'all realize this is a game-changing moment for Fabulous Jewels Events?" Jewel looked around the table. "I mean I'm *always* Team Lexi, Team Reynolds & Stanton, that once lackluster law firm, Team Anthony and Capri…so a little reciprocation would be nice! I was even team Rex and *Jermane*," She gave Jermane the side-eye. "When your marriage was on the brink of colossal failure."

"Jewel, my marriage was not on the brink of ruins," Jermane said quietly. She shrugged, "We had some little issues, just like any other marriage."

"Well, if you call Rex's potential porn addition and your flirtation with one stripper by night and student/slash Barista by day 'little issues' be my guest! But I digress…"

"Eh-um, is that necessary?" Jermane smoothed her hand over her flawlessly coiffed chignon and stretched her neck.

"Okay, maybe a bit too far. But ladies, all I'm saying is, I've been here for all of you. Why? Because we're sisters! Here I was thinking I was sharing a career highlight with my closest, dearest '702-where-my-girls at', ride-or-die, Ya-Ya sisterhood friends and well, never mind. That's fine. Go get your Migas, Huevos Rancheros…"

Angel took a deep breath and sat back down. "Okay Jewel, you're right."

"What?" they all said in unison.

Angel looked around. "Jewel's right. She's always supportive and here for us in her own wonderful and sometimes annoying way." Angel smiled. "We are proud of you. And that's really exciting news, tells us about your client." She placed her hands in her lap and leaned forward.

Jewel cleared her throat, "That's more like it. Well, we went to undergrad together and I was her big sister. I hadn't talked to her since undergrad. But let me tell you from what I remember, sister girl needed *major* work. I'm talking a head full of hair that looked like a hornet's nest and not a clue what to do with it." Her words fired like bullets from a gun at a shooting range. "The teeth were jacked up to the heavens, big coke bottle glasses with the fashion sense of a tree…but I, Jewel Antoinette Whitaker-Eastland, saw *potential* and went to work. With a little sparkle from her big sister fairy glam mother," she placed her hand on her chest, "Myra, I mean McKenzie went from walking disaster to um," she shrugged her shoulders, "dateable? She was always smart though. I believe she graduated with an almost perfect G.P.A. …"

Capri's forehead creased. "Wait, McKenzie Myles, I've heard of her. She's like a finance guru. Handles million dollar clients, especially athletes and celebs and been in *Black Enterprise, Forbes* and *Success* magazines. She's brilliant."

"*Really*? Who'd a thought? Anyway, I'm coordinating her nuptials! It's going to be pink, fabulous, and a very L.A. Affair! I can't wait to spend that, I mean their money!"

"Jewel, I'm so happy for you. *Now*, can we eat? I'm so hungry I was about to grab a roll off the table next to us." Angel waited in anticipation.

Jewel turned her lips to the side and took a deep breath.

"Well, I guess so. Only because your lemon chiffon blouse truly

deserves an audience." She pointed, "To the buffet."

Chapter 7 – Brunch Addendum

"So, how's everything at Reynold's and Stanton?" Angel looked towards Lexi.

"We're good. So glad we're over the rough spots. And since Capri has made those television appearances it's driven even more business our way. Never thought I'd see the day where I could pick and choose my clients." Her fork danced over her Mexican pastries.

"That's awesome. And who knew our own Capri would turn out to be such a natural on camera." Jermane dipped her spoon in her Chicharrones Stew.

"Well, it doesn't hurt that her husband's a pro ball player. That alone opens doors," Jewel chided as she waved her fork like a wand then stabbed her fruit.

"Uh, that had nothing to do with it. This was definitely a God thing and not at all in my plan," Capri chimed. "The calls have been rolling in every since I did that panel for that cable news show on the Texas voter registration laws. Television was the last thing I thought I'd be doing."

"We need women like you out there. I could see your passion and you could back up your position with facts. The way you articulated the law and broke it down so the average viewer could understand was brilliant." Angel said, "I was so proud of you."

Jewel paused, "Yeah, I, I agree. Capri girl, you did your thing. I was proud of you too!" She smiled wide. "So, did I tell you guys I'll have to fly back and forth to LA? Business class, at my client's expense? Do you know how long it's been since I've flown first class? I was having withdrawals. When I took Aja to Disney World, we flew Southwest. Now, as much as I adore Tom Joyner, to say the process was a little draining was an understatement. I mean c'mon! First come first come seating?" she said as sampled her shrimp enchiladas.

"Well Jewel, I would hate to think you were cursed to coach for the rest of your life," Capri snickered as she ran her fork over her Tostadas.

"*Anyway*, since I have this new client and it will be a major boost to my business, I was hoping I could count on my sister circle for a little extra support?" She clasped her hands as her eyes scanned each face in expectation.

"Okay, here it comes…I knew there was a catch." Capri raised her brow as she sipped her Mexican coffee.

Jewel cut her eyes. "I may just need a little help with the kids. Especially when I travel…"

"You need to talk to Lexi, I don't do kids," Capri quickly interjected, then stuffed her mouth with an Empanada.

Lexi took a deep breath, "Okay Jewel, you know I gotchu. Chris loves Aja' and little KJ. If he had his way, we'd have a house full of kids."

"Great! See this is what I'm talking about … sisters supporting other sisters. How would I make it without you all? I've got a ton of things to do and so little time! I had to call Brandon, my browologist, and for Goddess sakes, I can't go to L.A. with Houston Hair! And maybe, just maybe someone could lend me a few designer bags that are collecting dust in their custom-made closet? Jermane, Capri? I'm open!"

Angel rolled her eyes. "She's back alright. Girl, this ain't Bag, Borrow or Steal. Keep it up; you'll be right back in retail rehab. Remember, you don't have the check yet!"

"But I will soon!" Jewel twirled her fork and narrowed her eyes.

"Jewel honey, my closet is your closet." Jermane turned to Lexi, "You ready for the Links ceremony?"

Lexi kicked Jermane under the table. "Uh, yeah."

"The Links? You didn't mention that to me," Jewel whined. "And I'm your bestie."

"I well, it must have slipped my mind," Lexi cleared her throat.

"Wow, I'm appalled." Jewel placed her hand on her chest. "I was passed over again?" Jewel stared down at her plate as she gathered her thoughts. "You know what?" Her head shot up, "It doesn't matter because when I become the event planner to the stars they're going to beg, you hear me, *beg* me to join! Lexi you don't even like that kind of stuff. How'd that happen?" She whimpered as her face pinched with resentment.

"Um, well, it sort of just happened." She shrugged. "I sit on the board with a few members. Just been in the same circles and I worked on a couple of volunteer projects." Lexi's eyes moved between her plate and Jewel as she picked over her Migas. "Uh, where *is* that Sangria?" she said as she looked around.

"Whatever. It's that Tammy McCall. She's still holding a grudge after all these years. How was I supposed to know they were engaged? I mean really? I was minding my own business at that charity ball and her fiancé kept flirting. He even followed me to the restroom! What was that like a decade ago? Before her bypass surgery? Forget it! I've got my sights set on the Junior League." Jewel's nose turned upward.

Lexi rubbed her forehead with her hand. "Honestly Jewel, I really don't think that's the case. She's more mature than that. Just timing I guess. So Jermane, how's teaching, and your Dad, how's he enjoying retirement?" she said, quickly changing the subject.

"Wow teaching's a lot of work. Between lesson plans, meetings and grading it's tough." Jermane dabbed her mouth with a napkin. "Things are a lot different than when *we* were in law school. These students challenge everything. And they get into some hot and polarizing debates. But I'm glad I'm finally doing something I like. And my Dad, don't get me started. He's got this new girlfriend, Albany. Got the man going to the gym every day. She's too young for him, got him taking trips, skiing and doing all kinds of crap he never used to do."

"Girl, leave your Dad alone. Probably just what the doctor ordered," Jewel lamented. "If I weren't married I'd date him. That salt and pepper goatee, those bowed legs and ooh can that man wear a custom suit!" She fanned herself with her hand.

Jermane looked at Jewel salivating over her father with disgust. "Really Jewel? Get a grip." She rolled her eyes.

"You know, seemed like it was just yesterday we were meeting on that first day of law school." She shook her head, "Mmm, mmm if those walls could talk." Lexi sang. "Those were some good times."

"Well didn't seem so good then," Capri added. "That was a lot of hard work."

"I have fond memories." Jewel looked around the table.

"And to think that's where our Sunday Brunch tradition

started…thanks to yours truly." She crossed her hands over her chest.

"Guess you're right. Who said women can't be friends and support one another?" Jermane added.

"Ladies it's all about seasons." Angel raised her glass. "Yes, seasons. There's a time and purpose for everything under the sun." She sipped her drink.

Capri's nose wrinkled. "Uh-ah. Whenever you start to speak in parables something's up." She studied Angel's face.

Angel's lip twitched as she paused. "Okay, alright. You all know how involved I was in the last few elections. It really lit a fire under me. I mean my job in oil and gas has been a blessing but I could do corporate law with my eyes closed. I did some soul searching. It's not where I want to retire. There's more out there. I think, no I *know*, I'm about to make a major career change. I applied for what I think may be my dream job. It's practically a shoe-in. But there's a catch…I may have to relocate." She focused on everyone's face around the table, "to Washington, D.C."

"D.C.!" Everyone said in unison.

"But your life's here! What's in D.C. besides The President and First Lady Michele Obama, AKA BFF in my head and the *ultimate* Brunch Lady?" Jewel whined.

Angel took a deep breath. "Jewel, I went to Howard and *hello* my family's there."

"But I thought you didn't really like them?" Jewel quipped as her forehead creased.

"*Anyway* this job is not just *any* job … it's like a once in a lifetime opportunity. I mean I'd get to lobby on Capitol Hill. Guys, it's been so long since I've been passionate about anything, besides God of course. I sort of have the inside connection and I'm like 95% sure it's mine if I want it." Her voice punctuated her words with excitement.

Lexi rolled her eyes. "Okay, have to admit. I'm kinda hurt, disappointed…a little stunned, but Angel, if you're feeling that strong, you have no choice but to go for it! And it's important to see your family. People start to get older and I don't know," she bit her lip. "It's just important."

"I know. Believe it or not, I sort of miss my family. I don't talk about them much but I think I need to go home for, well some closure. I believe this is *all* God. It's a little scary but we have to be ready for change when we ask for it. I have aunts and cousins in Maryland and Virginia that I haven't seen forever. I'm torn, but honestly at the same time excited at the possibilities. Funny how you begin to appreciate the very things you've run from as you get older."

"Well, let's face it. You *are* getting up there." Jewel broke out in laughter.

"Funny. And Jewel, trust me sister. You're not too far behind me." She raised her brows. "Those Spanx-free years go by real fast, sister." She served an unapologetic glare. "Anyway, I really believe I can make a difference. I've made a lot of money in corporate law but this is bigger than money."

"How is that possible?" Jewel interjected.

"You know what I mean. It's a greater work. I'm concerned about women's health, tired of the rich getting richer and the poor getting poorer. " Angel's voice rose with excitement. "There're too many resources in this world for that."

"Fight the power!" Lexi raised her right fist.

"Okay y'all, I'm serious," Angel chastised.

"Wow, never saw this coming. The Sunday Brunch crew's breaking up." Jewel cupped her head in her hands then looked back up. "I apologize. It's just a lot to digest. I mean you know how hard it is to find the right chemistry of women? Not everyone gets a seat at 'the table'. Remember that God forsaken Missy, Mitzi…whatever her name was?" Jewel cut her eyes at Capri. "That reality show cast-off Capri tried to import into our circle? I could not stand her!"

"Jewel, if I recalled, you declared your adoration for her the minute she bought those purses from Dubai," Lexi clarified then waved at the waitress in the distance, "Can a sister get another glass of Sangria?"

"I thought you were driving?" Jewel quipped.
"One kid and a cranky overworked husband equal two glasses of something." Lexi took a swallow. "I'll just have to sit here a little longer."

"So Angel, isn't the crime rate like uber high around the nation's capital?" Jewel raised a brow.

"I may not live in D.C. There're great neighborhoods in Maryland, Virginia and the surrounding areas. Besides, I miss the culture, the Cherry Blossom Festival, Bus Boys and Poets and HU homecomings! I love Houston, but it's just different."

"Do people your age still party at homecoming?" Jewel rolled her eyes.

"Funny." Angel cut her eyes.

"It's a Historically Black College and University. Need we say more? The old people party more than the students," Lexi quipped. "Oops, did I say old? I didn't mean that. Angel, you're not old. The forties aren't old. Nevermind."

"*Oh, whatever*. The point *is* the Sunday Brunch crew as we know it will be no more! Guess this was bound to happen." Jewel threw her hands up in disgust. "SWV, Destiny's Child, The Supremes, OutKast, 702 *all* the great ones break up." Jewel sighed as her shoulders dropped. "Wait!" Everyone jumped.

"There *is* a silver lining in all this." She looked around the table, and added, "These groups usually reunite or get new members! Sure, it's after they can barely move, need the money, or no one really cares but," She looked at Angel. "All is not lost my sisters! All is not lost!"

"Jewel, you're not that great with change are you?" Jermane charged. "I mean get a grip, they serve brunch in D.C." She dabbed the corner of her mouth with her napkin. "Perfect excuse for a road trip. Wait that's kind of far, I meant a girl's trip via a first class flight."

"Here here," Jewel raised her glass. "Besides, nothing's gonna steal my joy! I still have my client! Last night I dreamt about a million floating dollar bills. It was just, just beautiful." She stared upward.

"So what's *Octavio* think about all this, he coming with you?" Jewel interjected as she sampled her shrimp Enchilada. "Mmm, has anyone tried these?" She closed her eyes for a few seconds as she savored the food. "Amazing."

Angel's smiled disappeared as she lowered a fork of Huevos a la Mexicana to her plate. "That's the *other* news. Octavio and I have parted ways…for good this time."

"What??? Double downer. You guys always break up. How long has it been this time?" Jewel asked. "You two are like an old soap opera. On again, off. Hot and spicy, then saved. What's it gonna be? Make up your mind."

Angel rolled her eyes. "Well, we're saved. No going back on that one. And I really prayed about it. Even did a fast and we both agreed it was time to let go. I have a peace about it." She held her breath.

Jewel looked around the table for reaction. "Wait a minute…did anybody else know?"

Lexi cleared her throat and slowly raised her hand. "Guilty."

Jewel's eyes shot to Jermane, then to Capri.

"Well…" Capri sang in a church choir tone.

"Are you serious right now? That's it!" Jewel stood up and placed her napkin on the table. "A sister can only take so much drama in one day. Excuse me, ladies, I need a restroom break." She turned away for her exit.

"Jewel," Angel called before she marched off.

Jewel froze folded her arms and slowly turned around. "Yes?" she said with her eyes looking away and her nose in the air.

"I'm going to miss this."

Jewel's lips curled in disgust. "Well, well…you should."

Chapter 8 – Blue Shield Blues

"So, Jewel supposedly landed this major client, one of our sorority sisters. But, the wedding's in L.A. She's gonna have to fly back and forth to plan the wedding that's only six months away." Lexi spread lotion on her legs as she sat on the side of their bed. "Chris, you listening?" By now, they would have both been laughing at Jewel's antics. "And Angel's thinking of moving to D.C. Did you know she and Octavio broke up?"

"Babe, nothing personal but I've got a slight headache. I can't deal with the Jewel stories right now. And no, I didn't know Angel and Octavio broke up. I haven't talked to him in a while. I've been working so much overtime I haven't had time to talk to anybody. Anyway, I just need to wind down a little. I'll check on little Chris, then relax in the TV room for a minute."

Lexi watched her husband as he started to remove his police uniform. She paused from wrapping her hair in a scarf, "Chris what's really going on? I mean for the last few weeks you've come in here, said maybe three sentences, spent a few minutes with your son, and sat in the TV room. You stay there until the middle of the night. I didn't get married to sleep in this huge bed by myself. Why can't you just relax in here with me?"

"Lex, please don't make this about you. Sometimes I get a little tired too. Besides, if we didn't insist on the private school for Chris I wouldn't have to work so much."

"Wow, I thought we made that decision together. And I wasn't trying to make this about me. When we first got married, you couldn't wait to get in the bed, snuggle, and just talk. Can't I be concerned about my husband?" Lexi's eyes darted back and forth as she waited for his response.

Chris put on a t-shirt and threw on some pajama bottoms, then locked his gun away. "Babe, look. I'm sorry, just a little rough today. It's just lots of tension out there. Ever, never seen so many people get into fights about everything — politics, gun control, Trayvon Martin, healthcare, marriage, two cops actually got into a fist fight today. I had to break it up. I just want to do my job. I thought I knew the men I serve with on the force. I respect them, and only expect the same in return. It got too heated today."

Lexi took a deep breath. She waited for her husband to turn around.

He came and sat on the end of the bed and looked her in the eyes. "Babe, it's a lot going on. Sometimes I think God's just looking down at all of us, wondering how far out of control we're gonna get."

She inched closer and grabbed his hand. "I get it. I'm sorry. I didn't mean to put extra pressure on you. But I know my husband and I know when something's wrong. Wow, I still love saying that word. *Husband.*" She grinned then rubbed his neck.

"I don't know, world's getting crazier by the minute. Guess having a son has really opened my eyes." He climbed on the other side of Lexi and placed his head on her thighs.

As he lay there, Lexi sensed the tension in his spirit. She wished she had a formula to make wrong right and solve all the problems of the world.

"Feels good babe." He grabbed her legs tighter.

"Chris, you're not by yourself. Sometimes I wonder what kind of world our children will grow up in. We just have to do the best we can and pray."

"I wonder if that's enough." He closed his eyes.

Lexi swallowed. "Gonna have to be." She sighed, and watched her husband give in to sleep. She'd never seen a crack in his armor. He'd always been her rock, the one to check *her* faith. Once she heard him almost snoring she eased out the bed. She went and checked on her son, who was still fast asleep, then slipped off to her office. She sat at her desk and pulled out her Bible and a small bottle of oil. She flipped the pages until she reached Psalm 91. She whispered the words then slid the Bible back in the drawer. She eased back into her bedroom, entered her closet, and then anointed all of her husband's uniforms with oil.

Chapter 9 - Somebody Stole My Life!

"You're in town right *now*?" Jewel's eyes grew big with each word. She took a quick panorama view of her house. Toys, dog bones, and other matter she could not readily identify littered the floor and several dishes had piled up in her sink.

"Yes, I thought I could stop by and…"

"No, no, I can come to you. The kids aren't here anyway, so this would be a perfect time."

"Oh, okay. Well, I'm at hotel ICON downtown. We can grab a bite here at Line & Lariat. I have a few meetings with some clients. How about a late lunch at around 2:30 p.m.?"

Jewel looked down at her watch. *11:05 a.m.* "Yes, that would be perfect. See you then!" Jewel hung up and made dashed to her bedroom. She paused at the hallway mirror. *Look at me, I'm a mess.* She ran to her closet, and one pile of clothes later she settled on a basic sheath dress, diamond stud earrings, and a pair of Loubutin pumps. *Wonder if she'll notice I had the red on the bottom touched up? Oh nevermind.* She was about to call the

Weavemaster but knew she had no time. *Can't ask for a credit and an emergency appointment!* She jumped in the shower, did her makeup, and slicked her hair back in a neat bun. She took a deep breath and turned to the side as she examined herself in the mirror. "Hmmm, not bad." She grabbed her leather tote bag, threw in her phone, iPad, and other essentials, and grabbed her shades on the way out the door.

~~~~~

Jewel pulled her SUV up to the hotel and realized she forgot to get cash to tip the valet. Bad enough she hadn't had time to clean out the random junk in the car, it smelled like Tinka. *Oh well.* She stepped out and handed the attendant the keys and didn't look back. When she walked into the lobby, she took a deep breath. She nodded and smiled at the concierge and instantly felt like she'd stepped into another world. *I just love the smell of a five star hotel.* She sighed as she tried to recall the last time she'd had a reason to stay in one. Then a flash of her pre-saved, premarital days of suitors flying her across the country at a moment's notice lit up her mind. *Boy, do I miss those days.*

"Jewel Whitaker-Eastland." A voice calmly spoke.

Jewel turned into the direction of the sound. "Myra?"

"McKenzie."

Jewel had to catch her breath. *This can't be Myra McKenzie or whatever her name is?"* She wasn't the chunky, awkward, girl with that hornet's nest atop her head. *She must have discovered a flat iron. Her teeth weren't even straight.* "Omigod. You look fabulous! What happened?" Jewel said before she knew it.

McKenzie smiled.

"I'm sorry, I'm just…"

She hugged her. "No, it's okay. Really, let's go get a bite to eat and I'll tell you all about it!"

~~~~~

"So you're marrying, Horace whatshisname?" Jewel's forehead creased.

"Hudson."

"Halitosis Hudson? I'm sorry, Horace?" Jewel's eyelids fluttered as she tried to picture the two of them together. *God bless their future children.* "With the acne and bifocals?"

"It's *Dr.* Hudson now. He wears contacts." She waved her hand, "…and Proactiv took care of that acne, honey. He does all the plastic surgery for the celebrity clients in L.A. He's the best. " She stuck her chest out.

"Noooo."

"Yep. That's the only work I've had done. Well, that and a slight nose job."

Jewel's eyes locked on her nose. "Nice."

McKenzie pulled her wallet from her purse. "Oh, here's our engagement photo." She flipped to the picture. "Number twenty-one of Jewel's Rules…if you can't find the perfect man, build one." She stood there, beaming, awaiting Jewel's approval.

Jewel gulped as her eyes nearly fell out of their sockets. Horace's sandy brown afro was gone and his skin was as clear as a newborn's butt. He was clean cut, sexy and downright gorgeous. "Wow, you two look stunning."

"Hate to toot my own horn, but I agree! Horace and I had always been friends. We reconnected years later at an alumnus social. How could a girl say no to this?" She held her hand out to show off a blinding diamond on her finger. "Jewel's Rule number five: Get the ring, by any means necessary! And nothing less than five carats will do!"

Jewel cleared her throat and slid her own ring finger under the table. "Right." She could barely take her eyes off McKenzie's exquisite emerald-cut ring.

"So, tell me about your Kevin." McKenzie placed her elbows on the table and rested her head on her hands as if waiting for a classic movie. "I just knew when the legendary Jewel Whitaker got married; half the sorority would be there. And two kids? Wow, I can't wait to have kids."

"Yes, um it was a beautiful destination wedding. With my bestie Capri Stanton, you know, the wife of professional basketball player Anthony Stanton. And yes, we were blessed — two kids." *So what if they're both from his ex, God rest her soul, and the story reads like a ghetto saga that'd sell out any chitlin circuit, but I digress.* "But enough about *my* boring life. It's all about you, the bride-to-be." Jewel laughed nervously. "So, what's the vision you have for your perfect day? How do you want to feel, what do you want it to look like?" *Deflect, deflect.*

"Oh yes, um, not really sure. I never envisioned getting married. I mean, let's be honest, I was quite the homely one." She laughed loud. "But now that it's here, I say the sky's the limit. All I know for sure is I want it eco-friendly and pink...lots of pink. But like a soft, almost salmon-like pink."

"Yeah, yeah...I get it."

Chapter 10 – Mr. Wendell

Kevin heard a knock on his office door. "Come in," he said, knowing it was former co-worker, Chad because of his knock.

"Sup man." His tall, lanky, bugged-eyed friend, dressed in a parcel deliveryman uniform came in and sat down. "You working through lunch again?" He dropped in a chair and slid a toothpick in his mouth.

"Naw man, gotta go to lunch with Bob and my new manager."

"Wendell? Wendell Wilson?" Chad sucked his teeth. "Man, that dude."

He had Kevin's full attention. "You know him?"

Chad rolled the toothpick around his tongue before he spoke. "Naw, just heard a few things about him. Kinda uptight and a little cut-throat. Former military. Just watch your back, man."

"Man, I just focus on being the best manager in the history of American Parcel Services and let God handle the rest. He'll give me the heads up if I need to know something. But you know me, I always sleep with one eye open and one eye closed." Kevin said.

"Guess it's part of the game." Chad stretched his tatted arms.

"Suppose so," Kevin quipped, thinking Chad was a little envious at his promotion. "Well man, it's only a matter of time before you come up. Keep doing what you're doing."

"Man, straight up. You deserved this position. And you was always looking out for everybody. You a good dude. Besides, I knew that snooty chick you married was gonna eventually get to you outta that delivery uniform." Chad laughed.

"Man you trippin. Nothing wrong with a come up. Look man, I got some work to do." Kevin waved at him. "And you do too. Let's try to catch up this weekend. Maybe shoot some hoops." He said as he eased out his chair to walk him out.

"Yeah a'ight." Chad got up, and when they reached the door, they hit each other's fists.

"Hey, thanks for lookin' out." Kevin nodded.

"Anytime." Chad opened the door and eased out.

Kevin sat back in his chair. Despite all the competition, he was confident he'd earned his promotion. He knew his attitude and work ethic gave him the edge. *Can't tell me God didn't open this door.* He looked at the picture on his desk of Jewel and his kids and felt a sense of pride, realizing how blessed he was. The one rang, interrupting his thoughts.

"Yes Sir," Kevin greeted his soon to be retired boss Bob Schaffer, after glancing at the caller ID.

"Hey Eastland, can you head down to my office in about five minutes? I'll introduce you to Wendell and we can head to lunch."

"Yes sir, be there shortly." Kevin wasn't looking forward to losing the boss that had given him his promotion. Bob was a fair man. But he'd been with the company since he came out of college. He went from a young, energetic, brown-haired kid to a laid back white-haired, man of wisdom. Bob was Kevin's advocate, and he'd schooled him in business and in life. Kevin was going to miss him when he retired. He knew it was going to be a change, but he was ready. Bob had trained him well and he wasn't going to let him down.

~~~~~

"Wendell, this is Kevin, Kevin Eastland. He's a good man. I know you're going to get along because you both work extra hard." Bob grinned like a proud father.

Wendell grabbed Kevin's hand and offered a strong handshake.

"Nice to meet you. Heard a lot of great things." Kevin made eye contact.

He nodded his head. "Likewise."

"So gentlemen," Bob smoothed his tie, "I don't know about you, but I'm starved. Wendell, you call it," he said in his raspy voice.

"Any good Sushi Bars?" Wendell asked as they walked out the office and toward the parking garage.

Awww, heck no! This bougie fool ain't making us eat some raw fish. I need some red meat!

Bob slapped Wendell on the back. "Now, Wendell, I know I said anything, but I'm from Waco. I need something with a little more substance. Like a steak. "Think you can work with that?"

Kevin smiled to himself waiting for Wendell's reaction as his stomach did back flips. *I'm gonna miss my old boss.*

~~~~~

"Uh, Kevin, you have a few minutes? Want to have a little one-on-one in my office before things get hectic."

"Sure, yeah sure." Kevin followed Wendell and walked past him as he held open the door.

"Have a seat, man. Office isn't quite together but the most important stuff's here." He extended his hand towards the chair in front of his large desk.

Kevin eased into the chair and quickly glimpsed at the walls. He noticed that Wendell had managed to get up all his certificates, degrees, and awards.

"Man, that was a great lunch," Kevin said, trying to break the ice. "Looks like you're settling in pretty good."

"Pretty well," Wendell corrected, then flashed a superior grin.

"Right." Kevin clasped his fingers together and rotated his thumbs. After a few seconds of silence, he cleared his throat. "So um, you from Texas?"

"Dallas. But I'm a student of the world. Went to the military, and they paid for my college." He crossed his arms and leaned back. "Got my first position with the U. S. Postal Service. Then went back to school for another degree, been moving up ever since. Looking forward to my role as Division Manager." He released his arms, then pressed his fingertips together and grinned. "Guess I've come full circle."

"Wow, impressive." His eyes wandered. "So, is this it for a while?" Kevin questioned, still trying to figure out the true reason for the meeting.

"Pretty sure, my wife likes Houston."

"It is a nice place to raise a family," Kevin quickly added. "My wife's happy here."

"You have kids?" He eyed Kevin's face incredulously.

"Yeah two. A boy and a girl, they're a handful." Kevin's face lit up as it always did when he talked about his family.

"So," Wendell said curtly, "Bob's a great guy, one of my mentors. But our management styles do differ slightly." He eased out of his chair and walked around the office. "Not much will change. I'm just a little more hands on. The buck stops here and I set the bar high. You know how it is. We've always had to work twice as hard..." He made direct eye contact with Kevin. "Know what I mean?"

Kevin remained still.

Wendell went and sat in his chair, then leaned forward. "Sooo, don't look for any special favors." He grinned slyly.

Kevin's eyebrows knitted together. "With all due respect, sir, I've always gone above and beyond in anything I've done. I don't look for favors. I'm in this position because I worked extremely hard *and* saved this company potentially millions of dollars."

Wendell threw up his hands. "Hold on, no need to get defensive. I'm certain you've earned this position. I just think it's critical to set expectations. Didn't mean to insinuate otherwise."

Wendell's words scrambled in Kevin's mind like a gumball in a machine before rolling out. "I understand, it's all about the team. If we look good, you look good. I may not talk much, but I let my action speak for itself. On that note," he stood, "If you don't mind, sir, I need to excuse myself. A pile of work is waiting back at my desk ..." He was about to smile, but kept his expression neutral.

Before Kevin walked out, a young lady breezed through the door.

"Wendell I…" She stopped as soon as she saw Kevin. "Oh, I apologize. I didn't know you were in a meeting." Her eyes darted between the two of them.

"Kevin, this is um, Heather Fleming. She's the new Administrative Assistant."

Heather walked over and shook Kevin's hand zealously. "Nice to meet you." She smoothed her wrap dress and smiled as she hugged her clipboard and a few folders. "Here's your spreadsheet." She handed several papers to Wendell. "I'll come back."

"No, no, I was just leaving," Kevin assured her, and then smiled warmly, thankful for her timely interruption.

"Heather's actually here to assist all the managers. So if you need any admin work feel free to utilize her skills. She's very efficient." Wendell nodded. "We'll get together later this week, Kevin, for some follow up."

"Good deal. Heather, again, nice meeting you," he said, glancing in her direction. Once he reached the door, he briskly walked toward his office.

Chapter 11 – Thought My Grass Was Green

Jewel bolted from Hotel Icon in her truck as beads of sweat formed across her forehead. *"Omigod!* Myra, I mean McKenzie stole my life!" She jumped on I-10 and pressed her pump to the floor. *I taught her everything she knows! She robbed my vision board and stole all my fabulousity!* Jewel shook her head. "No, no, this is not how my story is supposed to go. I was the one destined for diamonds, positioned for posh, blessed for bling." Her phone rang as she caught her breath, "Yes Kevin."

"I love you too babe. I'm at the store. We're almost out of toothpaste. I found these cool battery operated toothbrushes. I'm going to pick you up one. You need anything? You cook? If not, I can grab some Chinese."

"No, I didn't cook. I told you I had this meeting with a major client. It was really last minute. Right now I'm on the way to Lexi's to pick up kids." She eased onto the freeway.

"How'd it go? You finally get a client?"

"What do you mean *finally*? Forget it. Just pick up some toilet paper. I swear you need a TP fund. I thought I just bought a jumbo pack from Sam's?"

"Don't hate me cause I'm regular! I'm gonna stop at our favorite Chinese spot and pick up some dinner. Be careful, with your evil self, must be that time of the month."

"Whatever, bye."

~~~~~

"So babe," Kevin said as he shoved some Egg Foo Yong in his mouth. "I had lunch with the new manager. Just like I thought, a real uppity dude. Some Boris Kodjoe wannabe with a bald head and tailored suits. He seems cool, but I don't know ... something about him. He's kind of arrogant. Kind of get the feeling he's all about titles and degrees."

"Well honey, you're almost finished with yours. Thank God for your tuition reimbursement program. Those student loans sure can wear you out." She sighed.

"Uh, how would you know? I used a big chunk of my savings to catch yours up when we first got married." He shook his head. "I don't know how I let you talk me into that. I couldn't have been that much in love."

"Ha, ha. Anyway, I don't even want to think about what it's going to cost our kids to get through college."

"All I know is, I want Aja and KJ to have the best. And since I saved the parcel service company a ton of money they've been riding my—"

Jewel sighed and cut her eyes.

"I *mean*, they've been rewarding me ever since." He rolled his eyes. "Kevin, Jr. eat and stop playing with your food!" he said as he noticed his four-year-old banging the chair with the back of his feet.

"Aja, baby girl, how did your art project go?" He winked at his daughter.

"I can show you after dinner. I'm gonna win, daddy, because, well…I'm a winner!"

Jewel smiled, "That's *my* child. So baby, listen. I have this new client, and well it's going to require some out of town travel." She focused on her plate as she stirred her noodles.

Kevin bit his egg roll and chewed. "Cool. If it pays, sounds like a plan, when you say travel … like Dallas or Austin?"

"Not quite." She looked up, and said, "L.A."

"L.A.? Who in the world do you know in L.A.?"

"One of my Sorors from undergrad."

"Hmm. I know about some of your sorority sisters from undergrad. Remember? You used to tell me those stories. The road trips, parties, step shows." He drank some of his soda.

"How come you only remember that stuff? I also told you about the fundraisers, service projects, and the history. Babe, we're all grown now. Married, getting married and with kids. So don't even trip. It's a job." She watched her son try to grab the pitcher of juice. "Sweetie, let me pour it, in a minute."

"I just don't want you going down there getting all A-listish. As you said, you're married, with a husband and kids. Besides, do you really need to take this gig? Lately, we've been doing okay. I've been trying to take some of that pressure off you."

She paused. "Honey, it's not about you. I need this for me. I haven't booked a client in six months. As impossible as it may seem, I was starting to doubt myself. You take great care of us and I'm proud of your promotion, but this is a big opportunity. It's about business." She stood up to pour her son some juice. "Lexi said she would help with the kids if I needed it."

He examined his wife's face. "Sounds like this is a really huge opportunity and I don't want to be the one to stop you. I just don't want you getting any flashbacks. Don't' let me have to put you in retail rehab again." He laughed and smacked her on the butt as she made her way to her chair. "If this is going to help your business I'm behind you 100%."

Chapter 12 - The Fire We Make

Capri read the same sentence three times. She was trying to prepare for a news panel on gun control. Ever since her brief appearance on a cable news show, she'd become a hot commodity. Apparently, she was a natural, especially when it came to controversial laws or cases. Capri was going toe-to-toe with major legal experts and pundits. She was sharp, articulate, and could match wits with the best of them.

She removed her tortoise shell reading glasses and set them on the nightstand, then stuck her folders in her portfolio. She stood and reached her arms towards the bedroom's vaulted ceiling and stretched. She heard the shower running and the image of her copper-toned, muscular husband lathered in suds emerged. The shower water stopped and she smiled as several thoughts tip-toed through her mind. She lit a Marion P candle and turned on one of her Bruno Mar's playlists. As the scent of Cedarwood Amber filled the room, she eased her sweats off and slipped into one of her husband's button down shirts.

After drying off, Anthony strode into their dimly lit bedroom. A smile crept across his face as he nodded, "Uh-huh, Mrs. Stanton. I see you." She stood in front of the bed with her hands clasped behind her back with a coy look on her face. He walked over, still damp, with his towel wrapped around his waist. He reached his large muscular arms around her, "That's my baby," he said, then slid his hands around her waist. He brushed his lips across hers. "What did I tell you about wearing my shirts?" He whispered.

"You never wear this one," she murmured softly as their lips parted. She eased on the bed with her legs outstretched. Anthony climbed in the generous bed alongside her. He caressed her face, kissed her neck then looked into her eyes. "My wife is the sexiest woman I know. Love my baby." He watched her face in the dancing embers of candlelight.

She lightly ran fingers over his pecs. "Love you too. How about," she nibbled his ear, "you and I get…um a little fruitful," she whispered.

Anthony's eyes grew wide, and he was about to speak, but she placed her finger over his mouth. Capri gently pulled him close as she embraced his cavernous body. For the rest of the night they remained intertwined. As he liberally shared his spirit, and his mental and physical being, she did the same.

~~~~~

Capri woke up to bird sonnets coming from the bedroom veranda. She stretched her arms across the four-poster bed. "Umm," was all she could say after recalling the all-nighter with her husband. *Mr. Stanton kind of put it down.* A wicked and satisfied smile crept across her face. She slid from the covers and strolled to the bathroom. After using the bathroom, she grabbed the Turkish robe from the stand and looked in the mirror.

"Oooh," she said after eyeing the tousled mane atop her head. She finger-combed a few loose strands, brushed her teeth, then headed down the angled stairs. She smiled halfway down at the sound of her husband's voice attempting to sing Bruno Mar's *Treasure*. She snuck up on her husband and slowly wrapped her arms around his waist. "You got talent but singing ain't one of them."

He turned around. "Woman don't sneak up on me like that." He scooped the omelet from the skillet and slid it onto a plate. "See … I was trying to surprise you but you got to be all sneaky." He moved the flowers from the tray to the center of the kitchen table. He placed two plates on the table and poured them both some coffee.

"Umm, this looks good." She slid into a chair.

He sat across from her and smiled. "I think we hit a three pointer last night."

"Okay, just say grace." She bowed her head as her husband blessed the food.

"Actually, I think you hit several." Her eyes met his as she sipped her coffee.

He kept staring at her. "Babe, the first day I met you at that law firm, I heard God say, that is the mother of your children. Although you had that stuck up attitude." He laughed.

"No I didn't. I was trying to be professional."

"Babe, why did you change your mind, I mean about having a baby? You were so set on waiting another year?"

Capri shrugged. "I guess life knows how to get its way." She bit a piece of turkey bacon. "I handled a case once. A couple that couldn't have kids and they wanted a surrogate. Went through all this trouble and after all that time, the mother decided to keep the baby. They had every right to push for it but they just decided it must not have been God's will. They were heartbroken. Then one day I had a really honest conversation with myself. I had to ask God what I was really afraid of."

"I never knew you were actually afraid, I just thought it was your career." He eyed her with a curious stare.

"Honestly? I think I was so busy trying not to be a cliché…marry a baller, drop a baby. I never wanted to be 'that girl'. I wanted a child for the right reasons at the right time."

"What? You could *never* be that girl. I knew from the first time I met you at that law firm what kind of woman you were. I knew I had to work for you." He reached across the table for her hand. "You were worth it then and you're worth it now. Baby, you should know 'us' by now."

She eased in and kissed his lips softly. "Thank you." She paused as she sipped on her coffee and looked around. "You know I say it all the time, we're so blessed." She sighed, taking in the large kitchen. "And to have all this and not bring life into this world is just plain selfish."

He dropped his head for a few seconds, then looked up at her. "You never cease to amaze me." He reached and stroked the side of her face with the back of his hand.

After a few seconds, she grabbed his hand and kissed the inside. "Happy?"

"Ecstatic."

She watched his face. "Hey…you aren't tearing up are you?"

"Naw man." He jumped up and grabbed his coffee mug, then turned his back to fill his cup. "Sinus, you know it's that time of the year."

Chapter 13 – "Club" Office

Heather's perfume reached Kevin's desk before she did, but he focused on his computer screen. She rushed in as always barely noticing Chad.

"Hello Mr. Eastland, have your reports. And I reviewed that letter you wanted to send. I just made a few corrections, including the enclosure at the bottom." She rambled.

"Thank you, Heather." Kevin looked everywhere accept at her wine-colored wrap dress, which was a bit too clinging and exposed a little too much up top. "Darn, this computer! It's frozen again," he said as he punched the keys.

"Wait, let me take come look at it." Heather walked over and leaned down to see. "Ah, I think you may have a virus. You need to call IT to come and clean it out."

"That's the last thing I need. Oh Heather, apologies, this is Chad." He said noticing he was awaiting an introduction. He's one of our drivers here at the parcel company. Been with us a long time, a hard worker," he added, still focused on his computer screen.

"Nice to meet you," Chad said with a big grin.

"Chad? Oh, nice to meet you too." Heather smiled as she leaned up. "Would you like me to call IT for you, Mr. Eastland?" She tucked her hair behind her ear then smoothed the bottom of her dress with her hands.

"Yes, Heather, that would be great. And can you close the door behind you?"

Chad leaned forward. "Kevin, dude, I know you married but how do you even concentrate? Did you see all that? And when she bent over to look at your computer? Ah man! C'mon."

"You trippin' dude. Besides, we just had that training on sexual harassment. I'm not having this conversation."

"Dude, c'mon. She's like J. Lo., the Diddy years."

"Chad, not going there." He looked him in the eye.

"She dress like that every day?" He persisted.

"I don't know and don't care. Can we change the subject? And don't you have some work to do because I do?" Kevin grabbed some papers and pause to look directly at him.

"I'm officially on my lunch break." He leaned back in his chair.

"Man, you can't keep hanging out here on your breaks," He hesitated, "But other people *have* made comments at her outfits. Dress codes are a sensitive issue. I sort of feel bad that people are talking about and not to her. Maybe another woman or someone from HR may let her know in a tactful way what's appropriate."

Chad leaned to the side. "Word is she's kicking it with your boy."

"Who?" Kevin looked up from his computer.

"Ole' cornbread dude, your boss. Where you been?" He shook his head.

"Man I work, do my job and go home. Unlike some other folks that got time to sit up in my office." He sighed.

"Oh, so a brother can't come and hang in your office? I knew that promotion would change you. FYI – you didn't hear that from me." Chad placed his hands behind his head.

"Welp," Kevin said as he leaned back in his chair. "I hope it's not true. Cause nothing good can come of that situation."

Chapter 14 – Glory

"Okay, I'm only going to be gone for three days. Lexi's taking the kids to school and you can pick them up. So you think you can handle them for the weekend? I'll be back Sunday evening."

"Baby, I was raising Aja before you came along and KJ is a piece of cake. I got this!"

"I'm serious, Kevin. Aja has her…" She hung another dress in her garment bag.

"Dance practice on Saturday. Got it. I used to do all this by myself, remember?"

"Mom, I don't want you to go." Aja came in and plunked on the bed. She twirled one of her braids.

Not tonight. Jewel took a deep breath. "Baby look, I'll be back soon. You can have Daddy daughter time okay? It's only three days. I'll be back before you know it." *Boy do I need a break.*

~~~~~

When Jewel finally boarded the plane to L. A. and sat in her seat, she thought she'd died and gone to heaven. She stretched her arms across the seats. *Oh, first class how I've missed you.* She almost got teary at the smell of the leather seats. All she wanted to do during the first part of the ride was to close her eyes and take in the experience. She faced the window. *Um, a perfect Tiffany blue sky. This flight's going to be so relaxing.*

She smiled to herself then felt a little guilty when she pictured leaving her family. Aja's face was the saddest. *Guess you have to sacrifice something.* Jewel was caught somewhere between melancholy and elation when the captain announced they were close to taxing to the runway. She grabbed a menu and started to peruse her options. Oooh, Champagne, Caviar, Lobster Tails. Who says, 1st Class is dead?

They were about to close the door of the cabin when a last minute passenger rushed in and sat across the aisle from Jewel. She couldn't get a good look at him at first because he was wearing shades and a baseball cap and was turned away from her. *Naw, couldn't be, but I'd know the crook in those legs anywhere.* She waited in anticipation for him to sit down so she could get a glimpse of his face. When she saw him, her eyes widened as she almost gasped.

~~~~~

Since Jewel always thought of herself as a star, she'd never really gotten star struck. However, there were only a few stalk-worthy men who could make her seriously consider leaving her husband and break a number of the sacred "Jewel's Rules". And she believed she was sitting an arm's length away from one of them. She gave the man a side-glance from behind her *Vogue*. *That's him. I'd know my boo anywhere. Great, here comes Naomi Campbell wannabe and her flight safety ish! Yeah, yeah we know. Emergency exits, cabin pressure, oxygen masks. Hurry up and get out the way! Finally.* Just as the flight attendant finished and the plane taxied, Jewel's fantasy boo immediately threw a blanket over his head and turned toward the window. *Darn, darn!*

~~~~~

Jewel dozed off, and had the most vivid dreams. She saw vignettes where she was the lead actress in several Denzel movies. It seemed so real that she was talking in her sleep. She turned to the right and found her fantasy boo staring right at her, and instantly yelled, "Den-zel!"

He exposed a sexy smile with beautiful white teeth. "I was about to watch a movie, but listening to you was so much more entertaining."

She felt flushed as her hands touched the sides of her cheeks with her hands. "Wow, I'm so embarrassed. Sorry, um, Mr. Washington."

He laughed, "Sorry to break the news, I'm not Denzel. I'm Dennis. I get that all the time," he said as he chewed his gum. "Welp, don't mean to be short, but I'm gonna catch a movie." He placed his headphones in his ears and leaned back.

"Pssst. Pssst, Mr. Washington." She screamed in a throaty whisper. When he didn't respond she leaned over her seat and tapped him.

He took a deep breath, then removed one earphone. "Yes."

"I don't mean to be a bother, but I have to say, you got so robbed in Malcolm X, totally Oscar worthy." He stared into her eyes. "We didn't land on Plymouth rock, Plymouth Rock landing on us!" She uttered with conviction.

He sighed, "Ma'am."

"Ma'am?" Her neck snapped. "Do I look that old?"

"I'm flattered but I'm not Denzel." He winked.

"Look, you can't fool me. And, I was going to add, before I was interrupted, I believe I speak for the majority for your fans when I say, we'd like to see more skin. You know, a shirt off every now and then. Let's face it, you're not gonna have that body forever. I'm just saying."

"Ms., Ms..."

She melted at the sound of his voice. "It's Jewel. As in diamond, as in rare, as in, of great worth..."

"It was nice talking, but I'm going to take a little nap. If that's okay with you." He tipped his baseball cap and smiled.

"Oh, of course Mr. Washington, apologies," she whispered

He closed his eyes.

"Pssst! Hey."

He opened one eye.

"And FYI, I'm really not a stalker, so don't go putting me on some watch list. I'm a celebrity events planner." She whispered loudly

"That so. Well, good luck." He slid his hat over his eyes then crossed his arms in front of his chest.

Jewel quickly pulled her magazine back out and pretended to read until she saw a Naomi Campbell wannabe rushing towards her seat.

"Uh ma'am, can you please try and not disturb the other passengers?" Naomi wannabe raised her drawn-on eyebrow.

Jewel nodded and smiled. "I got it." She rolled her eyes when the flight attendant walked away. *Ugh, Horrible lace front.* For the next twenty minutes, Jewel was on her best behavior. She even tried to watch a movie. But knowing she was only a few feet from Denzel, or who she thought was Denzel, was driving her nuts. When she got up to go to the restroom she dropped a note on his tray.

"Ms. Eastland," he said once Jewel returned to her seat and picked up her magazine.

"Hmm," she said nonchalantly.

"You're not gonna leave me alone until I talk to you are you? Care to join me for a few minutes?" He pointed to the empty seat next to him.

"Oh no, I couldn't." She was out of her seat before he could say another word. "Now, are you sure Pauletta wouldn't mind. I mean the last thing I want to do is offend one of my sisters."

"Not at all, and trust me, she has absolutely nothing to worry about," he assured her. "You are quite interesting." He studied Jewel's face.

"So, I'm Jewel Whitaker-Eastland." She stuck out her hand.

"Yes, I gathered." He cleared his throat, "So Jewel…"

"Wait?" She pulled out her phone, "Can I just record you saying my name?"

"Uh…that would be a no."

"Right." She put her phone away.

"So," he took a deep breath, "You're from L.A.? Something tells me there's a story there." He leaned his head on the palm of his hand.

"Well, you know I'm an events planner. But I'm not just any events coordinator I'm sort of like…um…"

"Colin Cowie, David Tutera?" He offered dryly.

"Yes! Exactly!" She hit his arm and let her hand rest there for a few seconds.

He looked at her hand.

"Right!" She removed it.

"So Jewel, I'd love to continue this conversation," he said, hoping now that he'd obliged her she would leave him alone, "but I'd like to get some reading done." He picked up a bound notebook and opened it.

"Sure, but I just need to say…"

God why me? He turned to her and smiled. "Yes Jewel."

"Well, you see I, I, just…love you. I mean ever since Glory. You were so brave." She looked into his eyes.

"I really appreciate that." *Hey, might as well play along.* "Now if you could let go of my arm, I would really like to do some reading."

"A new script? Can you talk about it?" She sat up as her eyes opened wide with excitement.

"Uh, yes and no I can't."

"Right, gosh … you've been so nice." She shook her head as she stared at him. "Oh, do you mind if I give you my card, I mean in case you or Pauletta might need any kind of event planning in the near future. Wedding, anniversary? Red Carpet affair, divorce, I mean birthday…"

"Sure," he said in an exhausted tone.

"Great!" Jewel rushed back to her seat and grabbed a card from her purse. "Here you go, there's a couple for you and maybe some of your friends. So um, could I just trouble you for a little autograph, a selfie maybe?"

"Um, don't think that would be a good idea."

~~~~~

Jewel floated off the plane. "What a welcome to L.A.," she uttered as she strode into the airport. People were moving fast, and every so often she'd see a host of paparazzi trying to stalk a celeb and their entourage. Since she had had her celebrity fix for the day, she threw on her shades and rushed straight to baggage. She grabbed her bags and headed toward ground transportation. Before she exited the carousel she looked up and saw her name on a sign. She placed her hand over her heart. "Hello, I'm Jewel Whitaker-Eastland," she said, after walking a few feet.

"I'll be your driver, I'm here to pick you up and take you to your destination."

Thank you Jesus. Once Jewel reached the limo the driver opened the door and loaded her luggage in the trunk. Once he closed the door and they were on the way she raised her hands "Yes, this is my life!" Her cellphone rang.

"Jewel! It's McKenzie, so you made it okay."

"Yes, everything went perfectly. The flight was so smooth." She was about to tell McKenzie about Denzel, but didn't want to come off as star struck. *Remember you're here on business and you are a part of the A-list.*

"Okay, the driver is going to bring you to the house. Then we can head on to the Four Seasons."

"Oh thank you," Jewel said.

"First class all the way!"

I'm glad someone recognizes. Jewel glanced out the window and caught a glimpse of the Hollywood sign. She took in the breathtaking view of the winding hills and the coastline.

"We are sisters, but you're here on business. I know as the author of Jewel's Etiquette Rules, the undergrad edition, you wouldn't expect anything less!"

"Wonderful, can't wait to see you again. And I brought your own personalized wedding planner book." Jewel added.

"Ah, I'm so excited! I'm wrapping up with a client and soon it'll be wedding central!"

Before Jewel had a chance to respond, McKenzie hung up. Jewel tapped on the window and the driver opened it.

"Mr. Driver, I'm not sure if this is out of the way but do you think you can just drive me past Rodeo Drive?

Chapter 15 - Platinum Door

Jewel was so mesmerized by the California coastline, weather, and natural beauty she hadn't even realized she was headed to Laguna Beach until she saw a sign in the short distance. Her toes curled in her pumps as her heart skipped a beat. *Boy, when God opens a platinum door, he opens it! Lexi was so right about those affirmations.* Suddenly Jewel's hands shook and her nerves began to gnaw at her joy. *How in the world am I going to pull this off? I mean, I've been known to pull some miracles off but this is LA...*then she recalled one of her mantras. *Say yes, then figure it out later!*

Before she knew it they'd reached a gate and were easing into a driveway. The car stopped and the driver opened her door. Once she stepped out of the car, she just about flat lined. In front of her was the most breathtaking house perched on the Pacific Ocean.

Every fiber of her being wanted to pull out her phone and Instagram the whole scene to her girls but she caught herself.

Dazed by the sight before her, she snapped back to reality when the driver walked past her with one of her bags, headed towards the door. Before he reached the front door, it opened and out stepped a man in mirrored Ray Bans. She walked slowly towards the door.

"Now I know, this just can't be THE famous Jewel Whitaker."

Jewel squinted. "Horace?" He looked laid back and relaxed in a pair of jeans and a black fitted tee-shirt and some slip-on leather shoes. *Did he grow a few inches taller?* His golden tanned skin, a gift from the LA sunshine she supposed upped his sexy factor. She was distracted by his confident stance and beaming smile as he glided toward her.

Horace reached his hands towards Jewel and coaxed her into a hug, then kissed her on the cheek. "You look *so* good."

"Expensive cologne, strong arms, and is that a six-pack I feel?" She thought as she his sun-warmed chest press against hers. Slightly intoxicated, she pulled away.

"You and that Nia Long never seem to age," he complimented as his eyes took in her presence. "Um, um, Jewel

Whitaker, campus royalty, boy I'd like to meet the man that finally put a ring on it," he said with a sly grin.

Jewel blushed and laughed nervously. "Well, look at you." She playfully wiggled her wedding ring around her finger. "You don't look anything like …" *Uh-oh.* "I mean, you're so handsome…I mean…" She bit her lip.

"I know what you mean." He laughed, exposing what could have only been the most perfect veneers she'd ever seen. "Guess some of us pull it together over time. I'll be the first to admit, I was a big zero back in the day." He laughed. "I was all about the books. No social life, but it paid off. 4.0 GPA, class valedictorian, and a full ride to John Hopkins medical school."

He was valedictorian? Why don't I remember that? Jewel bit the side of her lip. "Wow, it did pay off."

He grabbed her hand.

She held in her breath. *Please don't do that.*

"C'mon, let's get inside." He stepped aside, then placed his hand at the small of Jewel's back and guided her into the spacious living area.

Jewel could see straight through the floor to ceiling glass to the beach. The space was light and airy with all white furniture. "This is stunning," she said as her body turned a full circle.

"I'm glad you like it. Kenzie tell you I pledged? Grad chapter," he announced as his chest puffed up a bit.

"No, she didn't … congratulations!" Jewel hugged Horace again and then jumped back. "So um," she swallowed. "When's McKenzie getting here?"

"Should be in about half an hour, she got caught up with a client. It'll be fine. Thought it'd be nice to have a little catch-up time with the infamous Jewel."

"Okay, please stop saying that." She walked towards the windows and peered out. "You wake up to this every day?" Her eyes locked on the patio, then moved out to the blue blanket of water that seemingly disappeared into eternity. *This must have cost a mint. I know my beachfront property.* "And who would ever want to leave this place," she said quietly to herself.

"Guess I have to thank my celebrity clientele for all this… and my skin care line."

Ca-ching! Again, how in the world did I miss this? She swallowed.

"I'll hook you up with some products before you go."

"Huh?" she said as she faced him.

"My skin care line. I'll hook you up before you leave."

"Oh, yeah," she laughed. "Sounds great." She walked a few steps and ran her hand across the baby grand piano.

"Yep, gotta dream big. I'm just getting started," he said as he watched some of his neighbors frolicking on the beach with their dog. "Oh sorry, you must be tired. Can I get you anything?"

Jewel felt her throat constrict. "Uh, a little Pellegrino if you have it," she said as she rubbed the back of her neck.

"Sure."

"While you do that, mind if I uh use the bathroom?" She looked to see if she could scope out the bathroom from where she stood.

"Oh, of course. There's one down the hall. There are a few more upstairs." He pointed toward the floating stairs.

"No, no, the one down here is fine." Jewel grabbed her purse and rushed off. Once she closed the door, she leaned against it. *Omigod, it's the double-win...fine and rich! Jewel, you really blew it, this could have been your life!* She started to breathe heavy, then her phone rang. She sat on the marble sink counter and the automatic faucet turned on. *Shoot!* She jumped up. Kevin's picture flashed across the screen, giving her a jolt of reality.

"Hey baby! Miss you already."

"Hey sweetie." She said, forcing an upbeat tone.

"You sound a little worn out. Thought you were going to call when you made it to McKenzie's?"

"Babe, sorry. Just getting settled in. I'm in the restroom and I just had a chance to get my bearings." She grabbed a washcloth and ran it under the faucet then dabbed her forehead as her heart slowed.

"Everything okay?" He frowned at the sound of Jewels voice.

"Yeah honey, great. That flight's a long one and I just realized I was a little dehydrated. Babe, I'm going to call you later this evening. I don't have much time, so I'm going to have to meet with the couple in about an hour. Everything okay there?" She pressed the damp towel against the back of her neck, then closed her eyes.

"Yeah, we're good. Oh, Lexi invited us for dinner. Chris will be home a little late but we're gonna all hang out for a little while. "

"That's good." She suddenly remembered her make-up removal wipes and dug them out of her purse. "That sounds perfect, tell Lexi thank you and give the kids a kiss for me." She opened the pack and began to wipe the make-up from her face.

"Okay. Just wanted to check on you and make sure my baby got to L.A. okay. Miss you already."

Jewel paused and looked at her reflection in the mirror. She took a deep breath and smiled. "Awww, thanks sweetie, love you too. I'll call you back later tonight. Love you." *Okay, Jewel Whitaker-Eastland. Pull it together. This is business! God gave you what you asked for, so don't blow it. You need to prove you can handle what you asked for, so you can get more!* She grabbed her travel-size bottle of mouthwash for a quick gurgle. She ran a comb through her fresh weave. She quickly put on a fresh "face" *and* her determination! She paused before she walked out of the bathroom.

Once she stepped out, she noticed Horace out on the patio with his back facing her, gazing at the ocean. She walked over, slid the door open, and stepped out. "Okay, I feel much better after freshening up a bit."

He turned around. "Well good." He handed her a bottle of water. "So what do you think?" He looked back at the water.

"Just gorgeous." She opened the water and took a long sip. "So is this where the two of you are going to live?"

"Um, for now. We may consider moving closer to L.A. since we both work there. Right now I have a small condo out there. Maybe keep this as a weekend home and build something else." The ends of his mouth curled in a smile. "So, what about you?" His eyes made contact with hers. "Tell me about the lucky man in your life?"

"Well uh…"

"Oh wait!" He felt his pocket. "My phone." He looked at the number. "Guess who?" He read the text. "McKenzie says she's going to be about an hour."

Great. Jewel mentally rolled her eyes.

"How about we take a little walk on the beach?"

Jewel was hesitant, but she hadn't seen a beach like that since her honeymoon. "Well, I'm supposed to be working, I'm starting to feel a little guilty!" She looked down at her pumps.

"No worries, and we can do something about the shoes." He pointed to a bucket of white flip flops. "For guests. You should find some size to fit you."

She walked over and reached in. "You know what? I just want to feel the sand under my feet. That okay? Galveston Beach is nothing like this." When she removed her shoes, she placed them inside the house.

He grabbed her hand and they walked down the steps. Once she reached the sand it was cool to the touch.

"Mmmm, this feels like heaven, so relaxing." She closed her eyes for a few seconds as the sea mist sprinkled her face and the breeze danced in her hair.

He watched her take it all in. "You know what? It's nice to see someone appreciate all this for the first time. I think you tend to take it for granted when you see it every day. You should have seen your face. It looked like heaven." He grabbed her hand and helped her walk farther down the sand.

She released it once they got close to the tide "So have you always wanted to be a doctor?"

"I believe so. I mean I was always fascinated by the human body. Never afraid of blood, and I don't know, it was so natural. Always thought I'd be a pediatrician but my mentor was a plastic surgeon."

"Hmm," Jewel said as she watched as seagulls hovered above the ocean. "Wow, what a beautiful boat." Her eyes shifted to the multi-colored sail in the distance.

"Well, we can take you for a sail before you leave."

"That's yours?" Her eyes shifted from the boat to Horace.

"No, I have something smaller but still pretty nice." He pointed toward the dock.

A boat too? Now what would Myra, I mean McKenzie, know what to do with all of this? Me? I'd be the First Lady of Laguna Beach, Dr. and Mrs. so and so..."

"And you, last I heard you were in law school?" he slid his shades above his forehead, awaiting her response.

Jewel was in a daze.

"Jewel, Jewel come back!" He snapped his finger with a laugh.

"Oh, I'm sorry, just going down my to-do list. Sorry, habit."

"I was saying, law school?"

"Oh yeah. I graduated, took the bar. Wouldn't you know it, after I invested all that money I realized I was an events planner masquerading as a lawyer. Go figure." She shrugged.

"You didn't need to go to law school to figure that one out. Everyone knew the fabulous Jewel was destined to do events." He laughed. "I remember you used to plan all those sorority and campus events. If it was a fabulous Jewel's affair it was going to be packed out."

Jewel felt his eyes on her and she turned to face him. "You noticed all of that?"

"Who didn't? Jewel, you were like that social butterfly of the campus. I mean I would hear all the guys in the dorm talking about you. You were an icon."

Uh, not sure I want to know about that conversation.

"Girls wanted to be like you. They copied your style, the way you talked, and all the guys wanted to date you. You were the prize, Jewel Whitaker."

She shook her head as if suddenly recalling how truly fabulous she was. "Well you know, I never *tried* to be fabulous…I was just being myself." She coyly pronounced.

"And that's what made you fabulous! I just knew when I got married I wanted my wife to be just like you." He kept his eyes forward. "Someone beat me to the original, so I got the next best thing!" He paused, then brushed Jewel's face with his hand.

Is that supposed to be a compliment? So McKenzie's a consolation prize? Her expression drained from her face and her spirit became a bit unsettled. Jewel took a deep swallow. "So um, when's McKenzie getting here?" she said, looking around.

"I guess another thirty minutes," he uttered, sensing her discomfort. "Why don't we go inside and talk a little more about the wedding. That's more her territory, but I think I know enough to get things started. Did she tell you we don't really have a budget?"

"Yeah, now that part I got."

Chapter 16 - Dance Dad

Kevin was thankful for one of many things when he married Jewel. She took over all the "Aja" weekend and afterschool activities, so he had his Saturdays to himself again. Before marrying Jewel, he'd been one of the few single dads at dance recitals, gymnastics, girl scouts, and a host of other duties. With little Kevin, he finally had the family he dreamt of. Since Jewel was out of town he was picking up his baby girl. She took dance and gymnastics. He stood at the back waiting on Aja to finish her tumbling. He looked at his watch, sure he was on time.

Aja looked up, saw her dad, then waved and smiled. He waved back and stepped back to lean against the wall. *She's no Gabby Douglas, but she's having fun.* The instructor dismissed them and the girls ran towards the back. As he waited with his arms folded, he glanced back at the door. Several mothers from the next group had walked in. *Heather?*

"Mr. Eastland." She burst into a smile as she walked closer.

Kevin barely recognized her nearly-bare face. Her tight fitting work attire was replaced with yoga pants and a t-shirt. Her hair was pulled away from her face with a head band.

"Hi, hi Heather."

"What are you doing here?" They both said in unison and laughed.

"I have a little one, Chloe. She's just starting. I heard good things about this school."

"Yeah, my daughter Aja's been coming for a while. She's been doing dance and wanted to try this. My wife's out of town, so I'm picking her up. My son's at our friend's house, so it's Daddy daughter day."

"Aww, that's sweet, a daddy's girl." Heather's face warmed with a smile.

He nodded, "Guilty as charged, you live in this area?"

"Yeah, a few blocks over. Welp, need to get to my little one … she's in that group over there doing the floor exercises." Heather looked in that direction.

"Oh, yeah, right." He said more alert, "Have a good one."

"Take care." She smiled and walked off.

He watched as she walked to the other side of the gym.

"Daddy!" Aja barked.

"Oh, hey baby," Kevin almost jumped out his skin.

"Time to go." She said, her arms folded.

He scratched his head and grabbed Aja's bag from her shoulder. "Right, we're going."

~~~~~

When the driver opened the door, Jewel eased out of the car, and then waited for McKenzie to arrive. She was calm and collected as they finally walked into the Beverly Hills Hotel for their meeting. They paused at the reception desk, "Hello, I'm Jewel Whitaker-Eastland and this is my client McKenzie Myles. We have a meeting with the Events Coordinator." Jewel felt so in her element and at ease in her sparkling "Events Planner in charge uniform." She thought her Mont Blanc pen peeking out of her iPad cover was a nice touch.

Moments later, a very tall, sophisticated brunette woman walked into the lobby and headed toward them. As Jewel smiled, she felt such a rite of passage. There she stood in her buff slacks and pale pink twin set, an outfit inspired by her current style muse,

Jessica Alba. Her eyelashes batted as she took in the décor and energy of the iconic hotel.

"McKenzie Myles," the woman said as she bypassed Jewel completely and air-kissed McKenzie on both cheeks. "Come, let's go to my office." Jewel trailed behind like a third wheel. Once they reached the woman's office the two women both sat down. The events coordinator slid on her reading glasses and reached for McKenzie's hand. "So, that rascal finally proposed!" She cooed as she inspected the bling. "Flawless. A pause in praise of the ring!" She placed her hand over her chest. "Now," she pulled her hand back, "tell me a little about your wedding plans."

"Well, we're thinking of a wedding with no more than two-hundred guests. Planning's not my thing, so I solicited the help of wedding coordinator extraordinaire Jewel Whitaker-Eastland of Fabulous Jewels Events." McKenzie rubbed on Jewel's shoulder.

Jewel cleared her throat and leaned in. "That's 'Fabulous Jewels Events - with Events that Sparkle Like Diamonds'." Her face was gushing with pride.

"Oh." The woman's forehead creased. "Nice to meet you dear. I've never heard of Fabulous Jewels." She removed her glasses, "And I know *everybody*..." She informed as she placed her glasses back on her face. "Are you based out of L.A.?"

Jewel's eyes widened. "Houston, but we're bicoastal," she quickly added.

The woman slid her eyeglasses back on. "I see."

Jewel's spirit deflated as she shifted in her seat. As the two continued to talk, she progressively felt like a sixth toe, unwanted and totally unnecessary. The woman went on and on about the various A-list weddings she'd coordinated and how important it was to have the right wedding planner."

Jewel finally cleared her throat, "I don't mean to interject, but we haven't discussed one *specific* wedding detail for McKenzie."

"Now, this is why I have Jewel!" McKenzie smiled and grabbed her arm. "Okay, so I guess the date is most important. I wanted to have the wedding in six months. I know it's extremely short notice but there's a reason..."

"McKenzie, sweetie, I adore you and Horace but six months, at the Beverly Hill's Hotel? Really? Do you know what the waitlist is for a space like this? Grant it, your husband is *the* best plastic surgeon in L.A., but I can't work a miracle, dear. Now, I can suggest comparatively exquisite locations. But unless there's a cancellation, this one is out of the question. So sorry, dear."

McKenzie looked at Jewel and sighed. "Well, I'm okay with another space, but Horace had his heart set on this venue. Only the best! That's his mantra."

"I understand but, honestly darling, even our cancellations have wait lists." She leaned forward. "Some A-listers have been booked before the ring – but you didn't hear that from me," Her wink slightly Botox impaired.

Chapter 17 – Dinner Debrief

Jewel adjusted her napkin after she slid into her chair. She exhaled as she perused the offerings at Morels. Her stomach said Seafood Fettuccini, but her hips were screaming Veggie Sandwich. She settled on the Cauliflower Purée, Tzatziki. McKenzie ordered the Nicoise Salad. Jewel was glad they'd stopped at the Grove, and thought the outdoor seating was perfect to debrief after the hotel meeting.

She smiled as she watched the busy shoppers walking by. However, she suddenly realized the little amount of planning she'd actually gotten accomplished. "Okay Ms. McKenzie, there's a few things we have to get done before I leave here tomorrow. Time's really short. But, can I ask you a question?" Jewel sipped water and smiled at the waiter. "Why are you in such a rush to get married? You aren't..."

McKenzie waved her hand. "No girl." She took a deep breath. "The truth?" Her shoulders dropped as she leaned back in her chair. "Somewhere in the back of my mind I think this was a joke. As if it was gonna all blow up. Like at any moment someone's going to come from around the corner with a camera and say, 'You've been punked! Guess I wanted to have the wedding before it happened."

Jewel's face cinched. "Really? Why would you think that?"

McKenzie shrugged. "A pattern, I guess. I mean, that's been the story of my life. Something great happens, then boom some disaster ensues."

"Wow, how can you say that?" Jewel smiled as the waiter placed the small plate of Country Pate' on the table. "Have you taken a good look at your life lately? May have been your story before, but not now my sister." She stared at McKenzie's perfectly air brushed make-up and flawless skin.

" Jewel, people like you and my sister Natalie, have been 'winning' all your life. This is new to me. I always knew I was something special, but it seems like it took the world forever to see it." She shifted her lettuce around on her plate. "As much as I've changed, I still hear the words that people have called me for decades...*goofy, failure, weird, funny looking*." Her eyes stayed focused on her plate.

Jewel cringed, knowing she was guilty as well. She remembered using some of those words when the girl she knew as Myra was a pledge. *Think Jewel, say something profound.* "McKenzie, you can change everything on the outside but you have to work on the inside." Jewel bit her lip and hesitated, "…and, you certainly can't be happy trying to be someone else." *Good one Jewel!* She gave herself a mental high-five for growth and maturity.

McKenzie's eyes narrowed speculatively. "Hmm, wasn't it *you* who said' fake it til' you make it."

Jeez, I didn't realize this chick was hanging onto every word I said. God, how on earth did you allow these people to follow someone so lost? I'm here to do a job, not play Dr. Phil. As she pondered a comeback, visions of a huge check did the salsa across her mind. "McKenzie, what I said was sometimes you have to 'faith it' until you make it." *Lord forgive me.* "Now, do you believe Horace really loves you? Because I do." She said channeling her best Jennifer Lopez as the Wedding Planner expression.

McKenzie's face lit up and she sat up taller. "I do. I really do. I mean he said he loved me because I was there *before* all the success. Guess I need to get out of my own way and stop second guessing."

"Well, then, enough of all this negativity." Jewel leaned forward. "It's bad for the skin." She lowered her voice. "This isn't a dream, but I am your fairy God mother! Forget the Beverly Hills Hotel. We can make magic anywhere!" Jewel paused for a reaction as McKenzie's eyes danced and her lips curled to a smile.

"Awesome. Jewel, having you here means everything. Horace had his heart set on that venue, but I believe he'd be happy with anything you pick! He trusts you."

Oh brother. "I have a few ideas. I'm thinking a fabulous home in the Hollywood hills or a winery."

"Omigod, we have a friend with a huge winery, and I also have a friend with a beautiful home in the Hollywood Hills. We could go to the winery tomorrow."

"That sounds great. Once we have the venue, the rest will flow. You'd be surprised how much I can get done remotely."

"I think this calls for a trip to Rodeo Drive!"

Jewel's heart raced and her hands began to shake. *Keep your wedding planner hat on! This is business.* "Well, I don't know McKenzie..."

"C'mon, what's a trip to L.A. without a visit to Rodeo Drive?"

Chapter 18 – Rodeo Drive Back Slide

Before Jewel could say "Louis Vuitton" they were pulling

up to Rodeo Drive. She held her purse tight against her arm.

Remember, you have not gotten paid yet. Be strong. You are here

in a professional capacity only.

"Oooh, Chanel," McKenzie announced with glee once they

exited the car. "Let's head there first."

Jewel's legs went limp as she felt her throat constrict.

"Right." She forced a smile. Once they walked in the shop,

Jewel's knees almost buckled. She almost became intoxicated at

the scent of the leather and the infamous logo. *Ahh, why God,*

why? After a few minutes, her desire to make a purchase actually

waned. Had this been even five years ago, it would have been

different. She was okay with just tagging along.

"Oh, this is gorgeous," McKenzie said as she spotted a

purse in a case. "It would be perfect for you."

Jewel just smiled, as the sales lady came from behind the

counter.

"Ms. Myers, you're back. So happy to see you." *Air kiss, Air kiss. They know her by name?*

A hint of envy crept up Jewel's spine. Once again, she thought of the days when all she had to do was get on the phone with a past beau and the purse would have been hers. Still, she kept her feelings in check. Then she thought of the black card she got from a long-ago ex who was a pro football player. That was until his wife got wind of it. *Jesus saves.*

"Okay, I'll take it." McKenzie whipped out her Black credit card. Once the saleswoman placed the purse in the white bag, Jewel silently longed to feel the rush of walking into any store and buying to her heart's content.

"Here you go." McKenzie handed the bag to Jewel.

"What? I really can't take this," Jewel protested as her eyes went back and forth between McKenzie and the bag. "It wouldn't be appropriate."

"Look, Jewel, I owe you. I was this nobody, a real train wreck of a person, you changed my life. I know I'm a client. But I'm also your sister and friend. Just wanted to say thank you." She wrapped her arms around a stunned Jewel and gave her a hug.

"Wow, I'm, I'm speechless. But I—"

"Jewel, I won't take no for an answer." McKenzie smiled.

Jewel's shoulders dropped. *God, what do you say, is this okay?*

"Well, who am I to deny you the pleasure of giving a gift to a

friend…" She grabbed the bag before God had a chance to answer.

La, la, God I'm not hearing you. I tried to give it back.

"It's the least I can do. You saved my life." McKenzie

began to tear up.

"I wouldn't go that far," Jewel said as they walked out the

shop.

"Yes. Literally, you saved my life." She grabbed her again

for a hug.

Jewel pulled away after a few seconds. She understood

McKenzie's gratitude, but her spirit nagged her all the way to La

Perla. But, after several hours and $15,000 worth of merchandise,

her conscience had taken a plane back to Houston. "Lord, I so love

my job!" she thought as she and McKenzie locked arms on the way

to the car and giggled like two college girls from back in the day.

Chapter 19 - Seaside Confessions

It was Sunday morning. Jewel awoke to a beautiful view of the sea outside her bedroom window. At McKenzie's suggestion, she skipped her stay at the Four Seasons and remained at the beachfront home. Serenity enveloped her as her eyes soaked in the mint and white décor. It was quiet, peaceful. No kids, dogs, or snoring husband. As quickly as she'd rejoiced, a small emptiness took over. *I actually miss all that.* She smiled as she stretched and sat up.

Jewel clicked on the television. As she scrolled through the lineup of Pastors, she realized that McKenzie had made no mention of church. Back in college, McKenzie was the biggest, for lack of a better term, Jesus freak on campus. She was in the gospel choir, and if nothing else, could sing the roof off any building. *Wonder what happened?* Jewel stepped out of the bed and touched the floor. Instead of a slobbering dog, she felt warmth beneath her foot. *Heated floors? This is ridiculous.* She poured a glass of water from the carafe and admired the fresh flowers on the night stand. *Now, this is the way to host a guest.*

She threw on her Turkish robe and walked toward the window. Despite all the ups and downs of her business, she absolutely loved events planning. It wasn't just about all the glitz, glam, pomp and circumstance; she loved the satisfaction she got from reaching new levels of creativity. She shook her head as she slid the glass door open to the small terrace. "I was born for this. Umm, Umm, Umm," she gazed at the morning sun perched atop the sea. *God, why can't everybody live like this?*

Her phone notification snapped her back to reality. She walked over the desk and retrieved the phone. She clicked on the text and saw a picture of her husband and two kids dressed for church. *Ah, they look so cute! He got them together.* Her heart melted. *Lord, if you would have told me I would have had two kids I would not have believed it.* She sent a quick text back, "Love you. Enjoy the service." Seconds later, her phone rang. It was McKenzie.

"Hey sis, you must be hungry, let's eat a quick bite and head to the winery so you can check it out."

"Sounds great. See you in a few minutes."

~~~~~

Jewel's mouth watered at the sight of the chef bringing out two plates of pancakes, eggs, fresh fruit compotes and sausage. *God, I must have a chef.* She was about to pause to say her grace when she watched McKenzie dig right in. She paused briefly and said a quick prayer. "Omigoodness, this is just heaven on a plate."

McKenzie smiled. "He's the best."

"So, where is this winery?" Jewel took a sip of her espresso.

McKenzie shook her head and quickly swallowed her orange juice. "Napa Valley."

"What? I can't go to Napa Valley, I have a plane to catch!" Jewel said, a little louder and more excited than anticipated. "I mean, that's five or six hours away. No way I could make it to the airport."

"Well, I was thinking you could stay over another day. I'm paying for it," McKenzie said with a dash of disappointment in her voice.

Jewel, took a deep breath. *Okay, God what do I do? She is a client. But I know Kevin is about to go crazy. C'mon, c'mon speak up.*

McKenzie must have sensed Jewel wrestling with her decision. "You know what? I'm so sorry. That was pretty presumptuous. You do have a husband and children to get back to.

Tell you what. In a few weeks we can take a trip down there. We'll dedicate the weekend to locking down the venue. You can still fly into L.A. but we can take a jet or drive down."

Jet? Jewel's eyebrow arched. She took a deep swallow of her coffee. "So, are you sure this is okay? I assure you going forward, things will be flexible. I'll be at your beck and call."

"Great. Maybe then we'll take a little trip out in our boat. Horace loves to show off his sailing skills…not!" McKenzie laughed. "Most of the time we have someone else manning the boat. We've got to get your hubby and the kids out here at least once."

"Sure, that'd be great."

"So, we have a little more time to relax before you have to get out of here." She took a deep breath. "So, tell me a little more about Kevin, your hubby. I can only imagine he's some successful entrepreneur that spoils you and your kids rotten. Honestly, I can't wait to have kids but I'm terrified at the thought of childbirth..." Her words punched with excitement.

Jewel coughed and almost choked on her pancake. "Oh yes, he's um a CEO at a fortune 500 company." She waved her hand. "Spoils me and the kids rotten."

McKenzie's eyes widened and she leaned forward. "So, how did you meet him?"

"Oh, um, I know this sounds a little cliché but he just showed up on my doorstep one day." Her nervous laugh punctuated the end of her sentence.

McKenzie laughed, too. "You are so funny, Jewel. So, when you had your kids were you scared? I'm terrified of childbirth. Wow, two kids. " She shook her head as she spooned some of the blueberry fruit on her pancakes.

God, I so don't want to get into the story about my kids right now. Love them to pieces but just not right now. Can I get a pass? "You know...I guess I was the exception. I literally felt nothing." Jewel shrugged and smiled. *Lord I didn't exactly lie.*

"Jewel, I can't explain it. You just really amaze me."

Yeah, I guess I amaze myself.

Chapter 20 – Clean This House

"Dad, I tried to tell you to clean up. But you wanted to watch Bravo TV all night," Aja said as she picked up some of KJ's toys from the floor.

"Aja, not now." Kevin pulled the vacuum cleaner out of the hall closet. He turned it on as Tinka, their dog, shot up the steps at the sound of the machine. "And I told you not to mention that."

KJ turned over with laughter on the couch. He thought Tinka's fear of the vacuum cleaner was the most hilarious thing.

"I should have called that cleaning lady," Kevin thought aloud as he pushed the vacuum cleaner across the living room floor. He turned it off for a few seconds, long enough to bark a few commands. "Aja, can you go in there and sweep the kitchen?"

"Yep, I do that all the time, and I can wipe off the counters." She put her tablet down and skipped to the kitchen. She grabbed the broom and started to sweep.

Kevin picked up toys and tossed them in the bin. He tossed empty potato chip bags and soda cans in the trash can. He had not even made it upstairs yet. The last he checked it was a disaster too. He paused to rub his brow and took a deep breath.

"Daddy, want me to load the dishwasher?" Aja yelled from the kitchen.

"Yes," he said without thinking. "Wait, no, Daddy will do that. Come help me upstairs."

Kevin took off upstairs to make the beds and clean the bathroom. He walked into his bedroom and headed toward the bathroom. *Jewel hates a messy bathroom. If this house isn't spotless she's gonna call her mom down here.* That thought propelled him into motion.

After a few seconds, he saw his dog Tinka sprint from the closet in a flash of red. "Tinka! What you got? Come here!" The dog always responded to Kevin's voice. He came back in with Jewel's pump in his mouth and dropped it on the floor. The flower accessory was now his chew toy. "No, Tinka! Bad dog," Kevin said as he tapped the dog. Then he walked into the closet. "Tinka!" Kevin yelled after noticing he'd had several of Jewel's shoes for lunch. The dog shot under the bed and made a beeline for his crate. "Shoot," Kevin said as he paced with his hands atop his head, surveying the shoe damage. "Jewel is going to kill Tinka, no she's gonna kill me!"

He headed down stairs to check on the kids and as soon as his foot hit the bottom stair, he heard smashing glass and KJ letting out a scream. "C'mon God!" He ran into the kitchen and saw KJ was holding his finger with blood gushing everywhere. He ran to him and grabbed his hand. "Aja what happened! Go upstairs and get the first aid kit."

"Where?" She stood paralyzed.

"In the guest bathroom under the cabinet. Go!"

"Okay, stop yelling." She stepped back and out the kitchen door.

Kevin saw the tears welling up in his son's eyes. "KJ, you're gonna be okay," He picked him up and put him in a chair. He grabbed a paper towel and wrapped it around the cut. When he looked at it, it was more than a nick but didn't look like he'd need stitches. KJ put his finger in his mouth. "It looks worse than it is.

Remember, we're gladiators!" He said thankful his son didn't actually release his tears.

"Here, daddy," Aja said as she handed him the kit.

Kevin wrapped KJ's finger and the disaster was over. "Okay, man?"

KJ shook his head, admiring his bandaged finger.

"You'll be okay." Kevin took a deep breath. "Aja, what happened?"

"Well, I was trying to help. I was loading the dishwasher and KJ ran into the kitchen to scare me and I dropped a glass. I'm really sorry, Dad, I was just trying to help."

He looked at his daughter and instantly felt remorse for yelling in a fit of panic. "Come here, sweetie." She walked over slowly. He grabbed and hugged her tight. "I'm sorry, it wasn't your fault." He kissed the top of her head.

Chapter 21 - Baggage Claim

Jewel knew Kevin would be waiting at the curbside as she left the baggage claim area. But she was wrong. When she walked out to the curb and saw no sign of Kevin, she was seething. *He knows this is one of my pet peeves…my father was ALWAYS on time when picking me up from the airport!* She was exhausted, dehydrated, and wanted to see her family. Her phone went off. *Finally.* "Baby, where are you?"

"I'm coming up to the curb now. I'm about five cars back. There was an accident on the freeway and Aja had to go to the bathroom. She couldn't hold it."

Jewel huffed and did a mental eye-roll. She stepped outside and spotted their SUV.

Kevin pulled the car to the curb and jumped out. "Hey baby." He grabbed her bags and kissed her at the same time. "You look tired."

"Gee thanks," she said as she opened the door of the passenger side. "Guess I am."

"Mommy!" Her kids yelled from the backseat.

Her eyes lit up and their voices gave her a temporary boost of energy. "My babies!" She opened the back door and reached over to give them hugs. They'd removed their seat belts as soon as the car stopped.

Kevin threw her bags in the back and climbed in the driver's side. "I'm so glad you're home, sweetie. This was too much work." He slapped her thigh. "What'd you bring us?"

Jewel smiled. "You are *so* silly. Okay, put your seat belts on so we can pull out of here.

"So, how'd it go?" Kevin said as they pulled on the freeway.

"It was a great start. Baby, that house in Laguna Beach was ridiculous. Right on the water. I'm gonna have to go back in about three weeks. When I envisioned my career as an events planner this is exactly how I pictured it," she said excitedly. "But it is good to be back home. I missed you all." She looked back at the kids.

"KJ, what happened to your finger?"

"Uh baby, nothing really. A small cut. You know kids. He's okay.

"Um-hmm." She eyed Kevin's face. "So, I know the house is a mess."

"No, baby it's not that bad, really," he said, halfway trying to convince himself. "But, I do have a little something to tell you. Honey, promise me you won't get upset? " He kept his eyes on the road.

"What? Something broke, burned up…say it?" she sputtered in a panic.

"Sort of…" He braced himself. "You know those Charlotte Olympia shoes you really loved? The ones that used to have the flower at the toe?"

"Yeah…" Her heart raced.

"And those Givenchy shoes with the studs? Well, I guess Tinka really missed you because she sort of tore up about four pairs of shoes." He winced and glanced her way, then back on the road.

"Each pair of those shoes cost…I can't! Baby, why didn't you keep him out of the closet? I don't believe it." She huffed as she stared at him in disbelief.

"Well, he never bothers your shoes," Kevin defended. "I don't know what got into him. Dogs are smart, he knew you were gone." He paused for the fallout.

"I just can't believe it. I'm going to beat his tail when I get home." She took a deep breath and remembered all her goodies tucked in her luggage she'd gotten from Rodeo Drive. Suddenly, her guilt was relieved. *The Lord must have known this was going to happen and that was his way of restoring my loss!* She took a deep breath and this instant calm came over her. "It's okay. It's only a pair of shoes."

"Really?" Kevin said in bewilderment.

"So, what else exciting happened?" Jewel asked.

"The usual," Aja chimed from the back seat. "Mommy, um um. Daddy farted the whole time you were gone. He didn't even say excuse me. It was disgusting! And he clipped his toe nails on the bed and didn't clean it up."

Jewel shook her head and let out a huge sigh. *No place like home*. She grabbed her phone from her purse and started checking flights for next month.

~~~~~

"So, honey, you know I'm having the Oscar Party next Sunday at Capri's house. I want to see Lupita Nyang'o hit the red carpet."

"Got it babe." Kevin bit his pickle and smacked with his eyes fixed on a rerun episode of *Two and a Half Men*.

"Kevin, seriously, you listening?" She bumped her leg against his.

"Yeah, yeah. Got it, you said you want tickets to see Lupe Fiasco."

Jewel signed deeply. "No fool." She slapped his leg. "I *said* I'm having an Oscar party at Capri's and it's a girl's night. You need to watch the kids."

He immediately broke his television trance and turned to her, "Nooo, uh-ah. I need a break after this weekend," Kevin protested.

"I told you about this weeks ago." Jewel fluffed her pillow.

"That was before you got this big gig. You can take the kids with you. Or we can all go, Anthony gonna be home?"

Just ruins the whole affect. She threw her body over to the side.

Chapter 22 – Oscar Buzz

"Jewel, if this is *your* Oscar Watch Party, why are we at *my* house?" Capri said as she watched Jewel gingerly place her custom programs with all the Oscar nominees in all the chairs.

"We have it here every year. You have the largest media room. Why break tradition?" she said as she smoothed her strapless formal gown. "And speaking of couture, where's your outfit?"

"I'm wearing it," Capri said as she looked down at her sundress. "I'm not putting on a formal to watch the Oscars at *my* house. Heck, I don't even know who's nominated."

Jewel brushed a loose hair from her up-do. "I'll have you know this is a stellar year. *The Butler, 12 Years a Slave*, Chiowetel Ejiofor and one word." She placed her hand across her chest. "*Lupita*. Omigod she is just exquisite." Jewel set out the champagne glasses. "Don't you just adore my pink sparkle punch? Those flecks of gold confetti are edible." She stepped back, took a deep breath and ogled her handiwork. "I adore those Oscar statues... I ordered them on-line."

"Okay girl, when you were growing up did you coordinate your friends' birthday parties? Never mind, I already know the answer." The doorbell went off and Capri headed to get the door.

Jewel did several fake poses on her 'step and repeat', "When you've got the gift, you've got the gift."

~~~~~

"She's in full affect," Capri announced as Lexi, her husband Chris, and their son came in.

"Hey sweetie." Chris leaned in and gave Capri a kiss on her cheek.

"Anthony's in the pool room," she said as she gave him a quick hug.

"Cool. C'mon son, we're gonna hang with the fellas." Little Chris, barely up from a nap, held his dad's hand as they walked down the hall.

Capri smiled, then turned to Lexi. "Uh-oh, where's your outfit, girl?" she said, eyeing Lexi's skinny jeans and sparkly top.

"Girl, I'm wearing something sparkly." She tugged on her top, then reached in her purse and pulled out a tube of lipstick. "And I have red carpet rouge on my lips. When I was single I could do all this extra Jewel wants. I love my girl, but ain't nobody got time for that now! I'm doing good to show up to these illustrious events she plans every five minutes."

"Okay, but get ready to face the wrath," Capri warned. "Especially since y'all didn't comply with the 'no hubby and kids code'. She made Kevin stay home with the kids." Her doorbell rang again.

"Hey girl," Angel walked in with Jermane and Rex.

"Uh-oh, another hubby violation. C'mon, ya'll are late." Capri hugged Rex. "Anthony's in the game room."

All the ladies shuffled back toward the media room.

"Well, thank you, Jermane! At least someone took my invitation seriously!"

Jewel walked over and gave Jermane an air kiss. She stepped back. "Exquisite, breathtaking," she said as she eyed her Calvin Klein one-shoulder floor length dress accented with diamond drop earrings, then cut her eyes at Capri and Lexi. "I'd expect this from Angel or Capri, but Lexi? I mean really, you always take my events seriously. "

~~~~~

"So when I get on the plane, in business class of course, the first A-list passenger I see is DENZEL! Omigod he is just as fine in person."

"Denzel!!!" Lexi and Jermane sat up and shouted.

"Yes, and I mean he would not stop talking to me. I think I practically booked a new client. Don't be surprised if I won't be tapped to coordinate Pauletta's next big bash." Her eyes lit up as she rapidly clapped her hands.

"Wow, that's wonderful, Jewel." Jermane smiled, "I'm so proud of you.

"I'm proud of you too, for that fabulous and flawless up-do you're wearing tonight. You are just always so classy and on trend."

Lexi rolled her eyes. "Okay, Jewel, we get it. I apologize for not honoring the Oscar Party dress code."

"But can we get a little pass? I mean Jewel we are in a different phase of life…kids, husbands, demanding careers. Sometimes we can't go all out with the themes," Capri added.

"That's all the more reason. We can't lose our girl spirit! You know I memorialize everything. You know every year I have the Oscar party and every year we dress up. What will this do to the optics? Nevermind," she said as she grabbed a hors d'oeuvre and put it on her plate. "I say anyone who did not dress up does not get a party favor."

Lexi and Capri shrugged.

"So, Jewel let's talk about something more relevant. What happened in L.A.? How's the dream wedding coming along?"

"Honestly, we didn't make much progress. I mean she hasn't selected a venue, but that house…" Her eyes rolled upward. "…to die for! They must really be rolling in the dough. After lunch on Saturday at the Grove we drove to Rodeo Drive, and it was like money was no object."

"Jewel…I thought you were supposed to be working," Angel questioned.

"Well, I was. I promise I didn't spend any money." Jewel bit her lip. "Omigod there's Lupita!" *Perfect timing so I don't need to confess about all the stuff I came back with.* "She's simply gorgeous…that blue. Work it!"

"I don't know, I'm not feeling the headband," Capri critiqued.

"Shush! They're about to ask who she's wearing. Lupita makes her own rules…Prada? A Fred Leighton headband?" Jewel reached for a tissue. "I'm having a moment. I'm literally having a moment." She put her head down and dabbed the corner of her eye.

"That's your friend," Angel said as she grabbed a carrot stick.

Lexi took a sip of her punch, "I know."

~~~~~

"So, I knew she was going to win," Angel said as she sipped on her punch. "Jewel, why do I have a sprig of lavender in my drink?"

"Oh, it's just a little garnish I saw on Pinterest, and well, I thought it was such a nice touch."

"I'm happy she won. At first I didn't want to see the movie but I was glad I did," Jermane said.

"Me too, but you notice the only films that win the Oscars are usually crazy or some pre-civil rights era movie? What's up with that? I mean I love Octavia Spencer and she is an awesome actor and I'm not going to even go there with Monster's Balls. Ugh," Capri added.

"I still say Angela Bassett in *What's Love Got to Do With It* got robbed. I mean did you see the body on sister girl? Angela is the woman and she can act. She was 'I Tina' for real. Made me what to smack Lawrence Fishburne! And you know I can't fight." Lexi laughed.

"I hear you. That's a long drawn out conversation. But we're getting there little by little. Cheryl Boone Isaacs is the first Black woman president of the Academy of Motion Picture of Arts and Sciences. And there's a major surge in indie films," Jermane added.

"We've come a long way, but have some ways to go," Lexi chimed. "But I'm proud of us!"

"Soooo, hate to turn the conversation back to me but…" Jewel said as she bit a cookie.

"No, you don't," Angel retorted.

"*Anyway*, I kind of think my client's fiancé is crushing on me. I know men have found me irresistible, but wow, he doesn't even try to hide it." She informed as she grabbed another macaroon. "I mean … why do I have to be so fabulous?"

"Jewel, just maybe there is an outside chance that every man isn't lusting after Jewel Whitaker-Eastland. Could be your imagination and you know you're a flirt. You can't help yourself." Angel warned.

"No, I have to beg to differ. When I first got there, he went on and on about how I was like the campus legend. And how every woman wanted to be me and all the guys wanted to date me."

They all were trying to hold their laughter in, but Capri couldn't help but burst out laughing, then Lexi followed.

"Laugh if you want, but it's true. Had I known then, what I know now." She sighed staring into space, "I barely knew the boy existed. He wasn't even a zero; he was like a minus or something.

Not even on my radar. But *now*...the man formerly known as halitosis Horace is not only gorgeous, but a L.A. Plastic Surgeon...caching!!!"

"I hope you don't ever say this mess around Kevin. God knew what he was doing when He sent you that man. Besides, it would hurt his feelings. Kevin would do anything for you. Although I don't know why," Angel sucked her teeth as she dipped her fruit in chocolate fondue.

"Of course I wouldn't say anything like that. But you can't tell me none of you has ever had a moment when you wondered what it would have been like to marry someone else," Jewel quipped.

Everyone was quiet.

"The only person I ever thought about in that way was Ty. You know, my high school boyfriend that died. But that's it. I didn't even want to get married. But I knew Anthony was my husband and I've never questioned that."

"Whatever," Jewel said. "I don't know what's weirder? The bride, McKenzie's like a clone of my former self."

"Now that's *really* scary," Capri nudged Lexi in the side and whispered.

"I heard that!" Jewel spat. "All I'm saying is I never knew the effect I had on people. It's like McKenzie took everything I said so seriously." She watched the faces of her friends for reaction.

"Never thought I would see the day when Jewel Whitaker-Eastland would become uncomfortable with a little 'Jewel worship'," Angel quipped.

"Funny," Jewel smirked.

Capri rolled her eyes. "Well, just be careful. Lots of strange stuff happens in Hollywood. You don't want one of those Eyes Wide Shut situations."

"Eyes Wide Shut?" Jermane's forehead furrowed.

"You know that freaky movie with Tom Cruise and Nicole Kidman…" Angel pointed her fork towards Jewel.

Jermane raised her brow.

"Uh, you know I watched that a long, long time ago. During my BJ era." Angel took a sip of her punch.

"BJ? What's that?" Jermane asked.

"Before Jesus." Lexi giggled.

"Oh, I don't think they're into anything like that." Jewel nibbled on a bacon rolled shrimp. "When we were in undergrad, McKenzie was that girl who'd talk about the Lord every five minutes. Worked my nerves back then."

"That's cause you were a heathen," Lexi charged.

"Anyway, that was the old McKenzie. She didn't mention a word about church or God." Jewel recalled as she crossed her arms.

"So, Jewel, you're telling us all this for what? You're the wedding planner not the counselor," Jermane sipped her champagne.

"All you have to do is what you're paid for. Separate the business from the professional," Capri added.

"Too late for that, she already told us the girl's business," Angel said. "But all jokes aside, Jewel just stay in prayer. It's business, but you know the enemy will try to use anything. It's obvious God's assigned you to this situation for a reason."

"Ooh-ooh," Lexi raised her hand, "I know why. Years ago Jewel messed a bunch of people up and now this is her chance to redeem herself!" Lexi teased.

Jewel narrowed her eyes. "You're just full of jokes tonight. aren't you? Why don't you go find your 21 Jump Street husband and head on home?"

"I'm kidding, girl. Geez, you're so uptight." Lexi waved her hand.

"But I guess you guys are right, premarital counseling is not a line item on my scope of services."

"And Jewel remember there's fine line between friendship, finance, and romance. I'm not trying to fly out to L.A. and rescue your butt under any conditions. Those days are o-v-e-r!"

"Uh, you don't have to worry about that Capri, that's what my husband's for!"

Chapter 23 – Player-Player

"So wassup man, how's the practice?" Anthony said as he rubbed the chalk on top of his pool stick.

"Man it's all good," Rex replied. "Father-in-law's kind of slowing down so I have a little more control over the firm. He's got this younger girlfriend. So he's no longer retired in name only. The firm's on solid ground. We just added an associate."

"So when are you and Jermane gonna have some kids. You're not getting any younger, bruh." Anthony walked around the pool table eyeing the balls.

"Honestly? We've always been content with the idea of not having any. We never really shared it because people think something is wrong with not wanting kids. Just didn't want to be judged. Our life is great the way it is." Rex sipped his soda.

"Wow. Ever? Just like that?"

"Yeah, I mean Jermane and I love each other's company. Society has its own definition of normal, but we have defined it for ourselves." Rex rubbed his wavy hair as he kept his eye on Anthony.

"I never knew that…red ball corner pocket." Anthony leaned down and shot the ball directly into the pocket.

"Oooh, that was nasty." Rex frowned.

Anthony stood up. "I'm hoping it will happen for us soon. We'll see."

"Y'all don't know what you're missing out on. I love Lexi but little Chris makes our family complete. He's my legacy," Chris said as he looked on with his son balancing his hands against his leg.

"I get it," Rex chalked the end of his pool stick. "Maybe we'll change our minds, but for now we're okay."

"I mean I'd give my life for my son. But this world we're living in right now really can make you question a lot. I mean, considering the stand your ground laws, school shootings, I think we may end up homeschooling in a year or two," Chris said as he glanced at the television.

"Still can't protect him from everything," Rex quickly reminded him.

"You're right. All you can do is pray, keep them covered. That's all we can do for all our children. White, black, Chinese, we're living in times when down is up, wrong looks right and all you can do is give your kids love, show them the way, and pray they make the right choices." Chris rubbed the top of his son's head.

"And, raising a son may be hard but I don't know ... I think I'd have to kill somebody if I had a daughter. I mean it makes me sick to my stomach when I see all the garbage on television and the way they glamorize the wrong women on TV. Our women may argue and fuss but they're not throwing things at each other. I just don't get it. If I hear one more thing about somebody twerking, making a sex tape, or fist fighting I'm gonna cancel my cable," Chris said.

"Man, you know the *Real Housewives* is Kevin's show."

"What?" Chris said.

"Yep, that and Scandal."

Chris shook his head. "That boy is special."

Chapter 24 – The Real House Husband of Houston

Kevin rocked back and forth. "Oooh that dag gone Ne Ne is sooo messy. She's wrong for that." Kevin heard Jewel drive up and switched from the DVR to the sports channel." He looked at Aja and put out his fist. "What's the code?"

She balled her hand and hit the top of his. "Don't ask, don't tell."

He winked his eye. "That's my girl!"

"But Dad aren't they just grown women bullies? My friends have better manners than they do? Except for my friend Mica. She said I had a donkey booty, whatever that is. And I thought stripping was a bad thing?"

Kevin paused to try to come up with a response. "Well um…" He heard the door open and Jewel's voice. "Go meet your mama."

Aja shook her head and walked out of the TV room.

"Babe, did you hear me call you? I wanted you to raise the garage door." Jewel walked in with several bags.

"Naw, babe. I didn't hear my phone ring. I'm so sorry."
He got up and gave her a kiss, "How was the party?"

"It was good seeing the girls." She shrugged. "So did you
all eat the casserole I left in the slow cooker?"

"Yeah, and your mama called my phone. You know when
you don't answer, she calls me. We didn't talk long but she said
something about coming to visit soon."

"Uh, yeah," Jewel said.

"Yeah what?"

"I uh, I'm going back out to L.A. in a few weeks and I
asked Mom to come help out here while I'm gone. This time I may
have to stay for a whole week."

"Jewel, you didn't ask if that was okay with me?" Kevin's
voice rose.

"Well, excuse me. Wasn't it you who complained about
having to watch your own kids while I was out of town?" She
locked eyes with him awaiting his answer.

He scratched his head, and replied, "Yeah but, not your
mama. I mean I love Mama Whitaker but she's just so nosy."

"Did you call my mama nosy?"

He put up his hands. "No, no. You know what I mean …

she just wants to walk around organizing stuff. After she leaves I

can't find anything."

"Whatever, babe. I just can't afford to mess things up with

this client. I mean this is a huge opportunity. And I don't want

childcare to be an issue. You have things to do and I'm not

trusting the kids to just anybody. So, as I see it, it's a win-win

situation." She raised her brow.

Chapter 25 – Car Ministry

The elevator was about to close when Kevin heard
Heather's voice. "Can you hold it?" *Shoot!*

"Omigod! Thank you Mr. Eastland. That Houston traffic.
And there was an accident on the freeway," she said, trying to
catch her breath.

"No problem," he said, keeping his eyes front and center.

"Wow, that's a nice tie," Heather remarked. "Got your
power color on today!" She chirped.

Then it happened. He glanced out her outfit. *Oh Lord.
Would somebody tell these women platform shoes and cleavage
aren't appropriate for church or work! She's getting a little better.
But dang!* His eyes shifted on to the elevator buttons. *C'mon on.
It's only three floors. I could have walked up. Something told me
to walk up.* He held his breath until the elevator door opened, then
exhaled as he walked out.

"See ya Mr. Eastland."

He rushed a few feet to his office, and as he was about to walk in, he heard a voice call out.

"Eastland."

He turned to the right and saw his boss, Wendell, standing there, looking at his watch.

"Morning." Wendell raised his coffee cup. "Made some coffee this morning."

"Oh, thanks, sir."

"No problem. FYI – I hate being the first one in the office."

Kevin gave a crooked smile. "Right, I get it, sir."

~~~~~

Kevin felt good after a productive day. Although he'd never admit it to Jewel, all he ever wanted to do was make her proud. Jewel's education was never a threat to him and after he really got to know her he realized God knew exactly what he was doing. She needed him too, and he'd helped her mature in a lot of ways. "God is something else," he thought as he remembered the day he randomly showed up on her door step to deliver a package. Now, he realized it wasn't so random. Once he stepped out of the elevator and was about to step outside, he realized it was raining. "Here comes traffic." He sighed.

Kevin took the glass-enclosed building tunnel to the parking garage and walked to his car. He grabbed the handle to his car door and was about to get in when he heard a woman, standing outside her car, talking on her cellphone. She was on the next level down but he could see her through the opening.

Go home, mind your business. Then he thought about Jewel. *If my wife was in trouble or stranded I would want somebody to help her.* He got in his car and drove down to check out the situation and quickly realized the woman was Heather. *Keep going, looks like she's okay.* Then his spirit would not allow him to leave. *Lord really? I gotta stop? I want to go home.* He parked his car and jumped up. "Everything okay?" He said as Heather ended her call.

"I don't know. This old car. Never can tell. I just need it to last a few more months so I can afford a down payment. I pray the engine hasn't completely gone. Hope it's something simple." She sighed.

"Let me take a look. Pop the hood."

Heather opened the car door and leaned in to pop the hood. Kevin walked over and tried as best as he could, to figure out what was going on.

"Try to start it up."

She sat in the car and turned her key. The engine didn't turn over and it sounded like a wounded cat.

"Try it one more time." After the last attempt, Kevin backed away and brushed his hands together. "Sounds like it may be your alternator."

"Sounds like money." Heather took a deep breath. "I just can't get a break."

"How long ago did you call the towing people?"

"About fifteen minutes ago. Go ahead Mr. Eastland. I'll be okay." She bit her lip and looked around nervously.

"You sure? I just don't feel right leaving you here. You can come sit in my car."

She took a deep breath. "Okay." Heather got in on the passenger side and sat quietly. "You really didn't have to do this. I have car trouble all the time."

"Well, no woman needs to sit in an almost empty parking lot alone." He pulled out his cellphone. "Let me text my wife and let her know I'm running behind."

"I appreciate it, Mr. Eastland, and I feel really bad for holding you up."

"Heather, stop apologizing okay? Things happen."

~~~~~

"It's times like these when you realize there are still good people in the world. One of my friends picked up my daughter from daycare, so I feel a little calmer. I'm not looking forward to this repair bill. Always something…"

"Heather, you have to be careful about what you say. If you use those words it *will* 'always be something.'"

She sighed. "You're right. But sometimes you pray and it just seems like things get worse."

"That's God just building our faith muscle." Kevin smiled.

She looked at Kevin, and one corner of her mouth turned up. "Mr. Eastland, I needed to hear that. You're a really decent person. Your family is really blessed. Sometimes you think there are no good men in the world. I believe there are still good men out there."

Her comment made Kevin's chest swell a bit. "My father was a little hard on me but I have to say, he made me the man I am. So, how's the job coming?" He said, trying to guide the conversation in a more professional direction.

"It's okay. I'm grateful, but looking to move as soon as I can to a better opportunity." She winced, "Oooh, probably shouldn't have said that."

"I understand and I won't repeat it. I can tell you're pretty over-qualified for what you do. But you do a great job. I believe because you are honoring this job God's going to give you a promotion," Kevin said glancing at his watch.

"I need something good to happen. Seems like when I get on a path to something good, I make some kind of dumb mistake. The only thing I have good going for me right now is this job and my daughter." Right after the last words had tumbled out of her mouth, her head dropped. "I did it again. Negative words."

"Heather, are you okay?" Kevin felt a jolt in his spirit.

She shook her head, but kept her face down. "I just want to give my daughter everything. I want her life to be better than mine." Heather's words were doused with sobs. She covered her face with her hand. "I'm sorry, I'm just a little tired," she said, still not looking up.

Lord, please tell me what to do. You know what You said about the appearance of impropriety. Now I could have sworn You told me to stop and help my co-worker but this is sticky. He paused while she continued to sob, waiting on God's instructions. He was about to reach out his hand to touch it back but when she finally looked up he snatched it away.

She took several deep breaths. "Wow, I'm really sorry I broke down like that." She wiped her eyes, "But it just seems like I have so much to do and so little resources. I mean, right know I'm staying with a cousin. I need work clothes. The only reason my daughter can even go to the dance school is because of a grant. I wanted her to be around positive girls. I really want her to be proud of her mother but right now I'm not so proud of myself."

Kevin reached in the glove compartment and pulled out some tissues. "Here you go." He still kept his distance.

She buried her face in the tissue. "Thanks, Mr. Eastland. I mean, I'm I try really hard, but sometimes it's not always easy to do the right thing."

Whoa…too much information. "You know Heather, if you are giving your best things have a way of working themselves out. And even when you aren't giving your best, God has grace. He meets us where we are."

She pressed her lips together and shook her head. "I don't know. He doesn't love me like that." She blew her nose again.

"Now what would make you say a thing like that? He's no respecter of persons. I mean he does not distinguish between his children. We're all special to Him."

"I hear people say that all the time. But I don't see it." She shrugged. "And I certainly don't feel it."

"That's the problem. You need to know it before you can see it. You have to believe deep down in your spirit." He placed his fist against his chest. "Heather…you belong to a church home?"

"Um, well not really. I just don't think I need to show up at church right now. I need to change some things."

"Who told you that?" He asked.

"No one, I just feel like I need to." She kept her eyes away from his view. "Some things I'm sort of ashamed of."

"Tell you what. You need to visit my church, Living Truth. You've got a special invitation. Anytime you want to come just let me know." He was about to reach out for her hand, but caught himself.

"Okay, I sure will." Her eyes met his, her faint smile revealing a trace of hope.

"You know what, I have a friend. He's a mobile mechanic. He owes me a favor. I'm going to give you his card and let you see if he can come look at your car. I know he'll give you a good deal."

"Well, I think I'm going to need a miracle. Matter of fact, that's what I call my car."

"Welp, God is in the miracle working business. And if you don't have much faith right now, I have enough for you." He reached in his wallet and gave her a card.

She took the card slid it her purse. Just then they heard the tow truck pull up.

Thank you Jesus. Kevin couldn't get out of his car fast enough. He looked at his watch. It was a little after seven. *Traffic is probably clear by now.*

Heather walked over and talked to the man in the tow truck. In a few minutes, he had the vehicle hooked up and was ready to take off.

"So, you gonna be okay?" Kevin asked.

"Yes, and thank you so much Mr. Eastland. That was really nice of you. I mean to wait." Before she knew it she'd reached in to give him a quick hug.

Kevin was caught off guard. Their bodies barely touched, but it still felt uncomfortable.

She stepped back. "Sorry. See what I mean, I shouldn't have…"

Kevin waved his hand. He looked around to make sure no one was nearby. "Don't worry about it, Heather. So how are you getting home?"

"The bus. The stop is right up the street."

"Lord please tell me I don't have to drive her home too?

"Okay, let me at least drop you off at the bus stop. It's pouring."

She looked at him and hesitated. "Deal."

Chapter 26 - Coming Home

After Kevin got on his way, he picked up his phone to call Jewel, bracing himself for the inquisition. He was on the fence as to whether to tell her about his co-worker's car problem. *Nothing to tell, right God? I'll just say I had to help a co-worker and if Jewel presses the issue I'll tell her the rest. Yeah, that's it. That way I won't have to lie.*

"Hey baby," Jewel said in the sweetest tone he'd heard in a long time.

"Hey, I'm finally on the road. One of my co-workers had car trouble."

"I know, I got the text. Come on, babe. It's wet out there and I want you home safe."

He had to look at the phone. "Is this my wife, Jewel, no fussing or twenty questions?" He laughed.

"I cooked too. Chili, hot and spicy just like you like it."

"You cooked? Whaaat? Wait a minute, what's up?" he said as his car hit a huge puddle.

"Nothing. Can't I just love on my one and only husband?"

"You better. This can't be Jewel Whitaker-Eastland. *My* John Legend *All of Me* muse. Nothing's ever *this* simple with you."

"Guess that's what happens when I take some extra time to pray and study the word a little. I know I give you a hard time, but every now and then I need to let you know you're appreciated. You spoil us all, and well, I don't want to take anything for granted."

"Wow, okay. I still think something's up. But I'll take this for now." He started to laugh. "Be home soon as I can."

"Bye, my little Hershey's kiss."

"Um honey…"

"Too much?"

"Yeah."

~~~~~

"Okay, Mama … sorry I had to get off the phone so fast. That was Kevin. He's on his way home. Anyway, like I was saying, I really need your help. When I came back from L.A. the first time, the house was a mess, the dog had chewed my shoes, and little KJ had cut his finger," Jewel whined.

"Kevin raised a little girl by himself. He can manage," her mother insisted. "I can't just show up like you're single. You're Kevin's wife first. He's the head of the household and you need to make decisions *together*."

"But Mama, I know what's best for our household."

"Oooh, that is a stupid answer." Her mother blurted.

"Huh?"

"Sorry, sweetie, I'm watching *Family Feud*. That Steve Harvey is the best host they've had, that bald head is growing on me. I kind of miss the flat top. I'm telling you I don't understand it when these people let the dumb people in the family play fast money. I mean you already gotta split $20,000 between five folk. I just don't understand."

Jewel heard her Dad yelling out answers in the background and smiled. Part of her wished she was sitting right there in the living room with them. She missed being a kid. *Okay stay focused.* "Mama," Jewel whined. "This is serious."

She sighed, "Jewel, I am serious. You are grown, married and need to take care of your own children."

"Well, what's up with grandparents these days? Aren't you supposed to *want* to come visit and spend time with your grandchildren?" She poked her lip out and dropped on the bed. "Used to be you could ship kids off to the country when you had to."

"Uh, times have changed. We have things to do! Who wants to sit around rocking on a porch wasting away? Don't try to play on my guilt, honey, won't work. I've spent plenty of quality time with my grandkids. I've raised a fine daughter, but those children and your grown husband are *your* responsibility. Besides, I got a bucket list to work on. You need to respect my schedule. You know I can't leave big daddy here by himself. The man can't function without me. Besides, we're about to go on a cruise. They're dirt cheap right now."

Jewel rubbed her temples. "A cruise? You didn't tell me you all were going out of town, what kind of cruise?"

"Out of Galveston. We were gonna do the Tom Joyner cruise, but that's when your Dad's Diabetes flared up. But we are going next year. We started buying our costumes and everything. Oh, I think that J. Anthony Brown is just as sexy as he wanna be! When he had on the purple suit in *Drumline* and was shaking it...umm, umm."

Really? "If you say so, Mama. Okay, I would not ask if it wasn't serious."

"Let me think about it. In the meantime, I need a favor. You need to talk your father out of buying a pair of those skinny jeans...He's been watching too much BET."

Jewel rolled her eyes. "My, I can't deal with that. But I'm flying out to L.A. in a couple of weeks, and this wedding planning is going to kick into overdrive."

"Okay, honey, now, can I get back to this not so bright family on the Feud?"

"Yes Mama."

~~~~~

Kevin turned up the radio and listened to the Majic 102 old school jams. Blast from the past. His head bobbed to the music and he reflected on some of his amateur DJ days. Although he was never a club person, he used to DJ to make a little extra change on the side. Then he thought about Heather. He realized how bruised

and negative she was. He thought about his own daughter and how

most men would have thought that being a single parent was a

chore. It was hard, but he wouldn't have traded raising his

daughter for anything in the world. He was glad she was a

confident, well-adjusted little girl in spite of his ex's instability and

passing.

He was even more grateful for Jewel. In spite of her over

the top ways, she was the Yin to his Yang … they balanced each

other out. And he could not have asked for a better mother for his

son and daughter. He took a deep breath. *God I'm really blessed.*

He still couldn't get Heather out of his mind. It wasn't anything

about her physically, it was her spirit. He knew brokenness when

he saw it. But it seemed as though she thought tight clothes and a

made-up face was her answer. He shook his head. *I will never*

have my daughter walking around looking like that. And she's not

getting any tattoos!

What made a woman seem so vulnerable and confused

plagued his spirit. It bothered him to see any person not

understand their worth. *This world is so messed up.* Even before he got his promotion on the job he was proud of who he was. He always knew he was somebody. He always made his daughter feel loved and that she could count on her father. He let out a deep sigh. He felt for Heather. He slid in one of his William McDowell CD's and his spirit got so full. He did pray aloud but somewhere deep in His spirit He asked God to show Heather who she was in Christ, to bless her where she needed it most and to show her just how good He was. Then he uttered the following words:

God, I'm not worthy. I thank you for a beautiful family, great friends, a healthy body and unmerited favor. I thank you that whatever comes my way, you have my back. I'm not ashamed to say I love you because you have kept me and you have kept your word. Whatever other test and trials may come, I will trust you.

Chapter 27 – Teachable Spirit

Kevin hadn't been sitting at his desk for two minutes before Chad popped his big head in the door. "Sup man."

"Man, you not working today?" Kevin said, noticing that Chad had ditched his uniform for jeans and a t-shirt.

"This is my day off. I came in to take care of some benefits info." He looked at his watch.

Kevin ignored him and turned on his computer.

Chad leaned forward across the desk, and asked, "You see your girl?"

"What are you talking about?" Kevin moved a few papers to the side and pulled out a notepad.

Chad looked around. "She's dressed a little different today."

"Man, I'm not focused on what that girl wears. I come to work and mind my business." Kevin fumbled with his tie, then wrote some notes.

"Whatever. She ain't showing *nothing* today."

"Heather's a nice young lady. She works hard and I'm sure she does not appreciate you worrying about her clothes." Kevin sighed and rubbed his forehead.

"Personally, I think somebody from HR probably took her to the side."

"Dude, did you ever think she was wearing all she had. She's probably doing the best she can."

"Man, how do you know?" He leaned back and studied Kevin's face.

"I don't know. She had some car trouble the other day. Sooo, I helped her. "

"Man she ought to with that bucket she's been driving to work. Looks like she was holding it together with a safety pin."

"You know how that is. I've been there. Praying something else doesn't break down on a car so you don't have to figure out how you gonna get a new one. I'm sure that's especially hard for a woman."

"Well, she must have hit the lotto or something cause she rolled up in something new this morning."

Kevin frowned. *How could that be? I don't even want to know.* "Man, look I got to go to a meeting in about half an hour. Do you mind? And I told you about just hanging out in my office. Seriously dude, it's not a good look."

"Okay, okay, one last thing. Ole girl is pushing a 230 Mercedes. It's clean, too, dawg."

Kevin looked up from his computer. "That doesn't make sense," he blurted out before he realized what he was saying. *Hope she's not selling drugs or anything.*

Chad stood up and shrugged. "All I'ma say is, no way she could afford that car on what she could be making here. And the plot unfolds. Stay tuned…"

"Man, for real. Get outta here. We'll catch up later," Kevin said, with his eyes focused on his computer. He finished up his notes for the meeting and dashed towards the conference room.

~~~~~

Kevin made it to his manager's meeting just in time. The only seat available was thee one nobody wanted … next to Wendell. "Morning," he said as he pulled out the chair and sat down.

Wendell was normally on time but running slightly late, so for him that was the scheduled start time. He opened the door and stepped aside to allow Heather to enter first. She always took the minutes. Kevin noticed that Heather was dressed dramatically different, he'd even use the word conservative. Her loose pleated skirt and blouse with a large bow at the neck covered more skin than usual. She walked in while avoiding eye contact with anyone and without the usual pep in her step.

"Good morning everyone. Apologize, I was running a little late," Wendell said as he placed his iPad on the table and straightened his tie. "So, just a few announcements, if you are taking any time off for the next several weeks, please get your requests in as early as possible. Also, if you have any travel reimbursements, please make sure the forms are submitted correctly. If you need help, Heather will assist you."

Heather jumped at the sound of her name. She lifted her head and forced a smile. Kevin's curiosity got the best of him. *Hope her daughter's okay.*

"Okay, if everyone could go around with your updates." Each manager, in turn, provided information.

Kevin reported last. "Our on time delivery rate for the last quarter was 95%, irregardless–"

Wendell's eyes widened as he clasped his hands together, and said, "Regardless."

Kevin looked at Wendell and cleared his throat.

"Regardless, the word is regardless," Wendell repeated. "There is no such word as 'irregardless'."

Kevin cleared his throat and shifted in his chair. "Right, regardless."

Heather kept writing and the rest of the team acted as though they had not heard the exchange.

~~~~~

Kevin sprinted out of the meeting. He wasn't necessarily embarrassed by his boss' comment. He was insulted. He was secure enough to take correction as long as it was done with the right motive. He prided himself on his ability to control his temper and not let people get the best of him. Above all else, he was mindful that Wendell was still his boss. He walked into his office and took a deep breath to calm down. Before he had a chance to sit in his chair, Heather knocked on the door.

"Oh, hey, Heather you need something?"

"Ummm." She looked around. "No, just wanted to see if you were okay." She took a deep breath as she held her notepad to her chest.

"Aw, nah I'm good, Heather." He smiled and was even a little touched that she had thought of him.

Her eyes met his. "Oh, okay. Also, I never had a chance to tell you thank you, I mean for last week." She looked around again.

Kevin sat on the edge of his desk as he tried to read her expression. "No problem." He was tempted to ask about her new transportation but caught himself. He paused as she stood still, almost as if she were waiting for a dismissal. "Oh, by the way. You look very nice today, Heather," he said, offering his approval of her more conservative look.

"Really?" She looked down at her clothes, then back at his face. "Thanks...I wasn't quite sure about it."

"My wife would approve, and she's the fashionista. She picks out my clothes." He touched his tie.

They both laughed.

"Well, gotta go. Let me know if you need anything."
Right when she was about to leave, Wendell appeared at Kevin's door.

Heather rushed by, "Was just clarifying some information for my notes." She tapped her pen on her notepad.

Wendell smiled. "Yes, we need our minutes accurate. Have a good day," he said as she slinked by.

"Thought you might need this." Wendell handed Kevin a book on business correspondence. "Just making sure we are our best selves."

Kevin nodded his head. "Appreciate it..." he hesitated, "Sir."

"No problem. There's no 'I' in team. We have to look out for each other."

Kevin nodded slowly. "Right."

Chapter 28 – Wedding Central

Jewel smiled as he opened the e-mail from McKenzie. She was finally getting into bride mode. She'd sent Jewel links to three wineries in Napa Valley and a host of wedding dresses she liked. And finally, the first draft of the guest list. She'd also hinted to pushing out the wedding date to give them a little more time. She continued down the checklist of the McKenzie planner, checking off items with glee. She sketched in McKenzie's wedding colors…buff, white with a just a hint of pink, inspired by Sabrina and Jason in the movie *Jumping the Broom*. She made a reminder to check on the McKenzie wedding website which was under major construction.

As much as Jewel hated the extreme ups and downs of events planning, nothing made her smile like planning a bride's wedding. With all the pending travel, Jewel was trying to be as organized as possible. She got up from the computer and entered her walk-in closet. She had managed to unpack all her "gifts" from the last trip without notice, which more than softened the blow from Tinka's shoe massacre. She wanted to get angry at the thought, but Tinka sat in the doorway, gazing upward with those big brown eyes.

She turned on *Happy* by Pharrell from her phone app and danced as she started to pack. Pretty soon, Aja heard her favorite song and came in the room singing. She and Jewel grabbed hands and they moved around the large closet, sang, and fell out on the floor. Jewel had to catch her breath as she stood. "Okay, young lady, did you finish your homework?" she asked as she kissed Aja on the forehead.

"Yes ma'am."

Aja walked over grabbed several costume necklaces off the island and piled them around her neck. Then she draped a vintage Burberry scarf loosely over the necklaces.

"KJ sleep?" Jewel asked as she tugged on the scarf.

"Yep." Aja dropped down to Jewel's vanity bench. She faced the mirror as she sniffed several perfume bottles. Then she sighed. "Mom, I think I hate weddings."

Jewel turned around. "What? Weddings are beautiful. That's when a man and a woman stand in front of God, their family, and friends and pledge eternal love. It's the most romantic and beautiful thing and I get to be a part of it. Doesn't that sound really special?"

"Yes. I guess it's not really the wedding I hate. I guess I don't like anything that takes you away from me, especially when you have to go out of town," she said, looking downward.

Jewel clutched the dress to her chest and paused before she spoke. "Aja, you never said anything like that before." She walked toward Aja and knelt in front of her. She placed her hands on her knees and looked in her daughter's face. "Sweetie, this is my job. It won't be like this every time. But it's really important to mommy. You want me to do my best don't you?" she said as she sat next to her on the vanity bench and brushed her thick hair away from her face. "I need you to look out for your brother…and your Dad."

Aja sat there, silent for a few seconds. "Mom, I know I'm ten almost going on eleven but I still need somebody to take care of me. And, well Pop Warner cheerleading tryouts are coming up soon and I need you to help me."

"I can help you, don't worry about that. Okay?" She touched Aja's chin. "Hey, how about we get Grandma Whitaker to come down?"

Aja's face lit into a smile. "Yeah, I'd like that. She's always so much fun. And I bet she could help me with my tryouts."

Jewels eyes sparkled, "Oh yeah, there's not much Grandma Whitaker can't do!"

Chapter 29 – Full House

Kevin was in blissful slumber. He awakened to the heavenly smell of bacon and eggs. "Mmmm, my baby in the kitchen making her king breakfast before she heads out of town." He stretched and yawned from his generous bed. *No dog, no kids... Perfect.*

Although it felt good to sleep in on Saturday, he suddenly realized this scene was a little too perfect. He eased out of the bed, slid on his slippers, and walked out to the top of the stairs. He heard Jewel's voice laughing. She must be on the phone. He walked halfway down the steps. *Awww, heck no!*

"That my handsome son-in-law?" A voice in the living room called.

Busted. "Uh, yeah Mama Whitaker, "he croaked.

"Dad, c'mon. Grandma made a big breakfast with homemade biscuits," Aja yelled.

He paused for a James Evans moment. "I'm coming, I need to throw on my robe." He clenched his teeth, trying to temper the boiling frustration in his spirit. *I'ma have a talk with Jewel before she leaves...after breakfast.*

~~~~~

Kevin turned up the radio. He wasn't ignoring Jewel, but he was still hot as fish grease.

"C'mon Kevin, I can't get on that plane knowing you're mad at me. I mean, I didn't know what else to do."

"Oh please, it's classic Jewel. Act first and seek forgiveness later. This client is not the end all to be all."

Jewel stared at the side of Kevin's head as he drove up the ramp to the airport. "Maybe not for you, Kevin. Granted, this isn't the ideal situation but it's a major opportunity. I, for one, do not want to blow it and I want to feel at peace, knowing my home and family will be in order while I'm gone."

Kevin took a deep breath and kept his eyes focused forward. Although she was partially right he didn't feel like giving in at the moment. But since she was getting on the plane, he didn't want the guilt of anything happening and her leaving on a bad note. "It's okay, sweetie. Don't worry about it. But I will say this. If you think you're gonna be jumping on a plane every five minutes for some hotsy-totsy fru-fru client and neglect your kids, you have another think coming!" He opened the door without giving her a chance to respond.

Jewel paused before she got out of the car. "Is he serious?" Before she knew it she had slammed the door and rushed to the back where he was unloading her luggage. "I think you are taking this submission thing a little too far. I had a life before I met you, Kevin Eastland! I'm somebody!"

"What the heck are you talking about?" He paused and looked at her.

"I know what this is about. You've been enjoying this little 'head of the household' role. You've been enjoying being the breadwinner, writing the checks, and controlling the money. You know what? I can make money, too."

"Really? I just thought you were good at spending it." He knew he'd struck a nerve, but didn't care.

"Oh, oh, so you want to go there," she said.

A police officer was walking toward Kevin, about to tell him he had to move the car. "Sir, are you finished dropping off the passenger?"

Kevin looked at the officer. "Yes sir."

Jewel and Kevin both paused momentarily. They never parted ways without at least a kiss goodbye. He sighed, then leaned in and kissed his wife. She allowed him to kiss her, but tightened her lips. "Love you."

She looked at him and wanted to say the same but her stubbornness won.

"Sir," the police officer said, waiting.

Kevin hesitated, but shut his trunk and jumped in his car. Although he was not completely wrong, his spirit nagged him all the way home. When he finally walked through the door, the aroma of ox tails, candied yams, cabbage, and cornbread greeted him at the door. The house was spotless. KJ was on the couch playing a game and Aja was working on her homework.

"Hey, son-in-law. Got your food in the microwave. Why don't you go upstairs, get cleaned up, and then have a good meal."

He smiled as his guilt was consuming him. He loved his mother in-law but resented the notion that he could not manage things while Jewel was away. But in that moment he was glad Mama Whitaker was there. Especially when he smelled those Ox

Tails. Jewel would never cook them for him, so he was going to enjoy this. And Mama Whitaker could throw down.

"Yes Ma'am," he said, realizing he had been acting less than welcoming earlier in the day. "Um, Mama Whitaker," he said before he started up the first step.

She waved her hand as she stood in the kitchen doorway. "Uh, didn't I say go upstairs and get cleaned up?" Her voice was warm like honey. "No, come on before this food gets cold. Especially, after I've done all this work…"

"Yes Ma'am, be right back."

She turned away, humming *I Need Just a Little More Jesus* by Erica Campbell, and went back into the kitchen.

Chapter 30 – Hey Hollywood

Jewel was exhausted, so she practically slept all the way to L.A. This time the driver took her to L'Ermitage in Beverly Hills. Staying at the hotel would keep her focused and in professional planning mode. As soon as she checked in, she instantly exhaled at the suite's neutral colors and plush décor. Flesh tulips and luxury candles awaited her in the large bathroom, and a small but beautiful terrace provided fabulous natural light.

She slid the glass door open and took a few minutes to rest on the outdoor couch. Then immediately sent a text to Kevin, letting him know she'd made it to L.A. safely and called her mother to check on the kids. She couldn't help but send a few Instagram shots to her girls with the comment: *My office for the week – smile.*

After a good meal and a solid night's rest, her goal was to wake up energized to hit the ground running early Monday. A week seemed like a long time, but she and McKenzie had an endless list of chores. Failure was not an option, especially after

her husband's rant on the way to the airport. *Play time is over!*
After ordering room service and catching up on an episode of
Fashion Police her eyelids gave way.

~~~~~

Jewel's phone alarm, blared, and her eyes flew open. She
jumped out of bed and stretched, then went straight to the shower.
"No husband banging on the door or kids to get ready," she
thought as the pulsating water from the extra-large showerhead hit
her face. She inhaled the fragrant body wash as a rich thick lather
covered her body. *Today it's all about the bride. Focus, Jewel.*
Once she stepped out the shower and dried off, she slid on her
cream slacks, with a matching top from Hugo Boss. It was chic,
well-tailored, and comfortable. After getting dressed, she sat on her
bed, read a few scriptures, and said a few prayers.

Dear Jesus,

Thank you for getting me here safely. My goal is to make
McKenzie feel special. I realize a wedding isn't a marriage but
each bride (especially one with an unlimited budget) should have
her day. Give me the wisdom, organization, focus, and
professionalism to exceed this couple's expectations. Above all, I

pray that Your will be done concerning this entire experience. In the meantime, I apologize for not getting my husband's permission before I asked my mother to come. But I just thought I was doing what was best. Kevin's a good man. If I did anything to offend him, I'm sorry. God You know I'm spoiled and I'm still working on that submission thing. I am praying for a willing spirit, a yielded heart, divine instructions, provision, and protection.

In Jesus,

Amen.

Chapter 31 – Ox Tail Love

Kevin let out a loud belch as he finished his third plate of food. "Mama Whitaker, you put your foot in those ox tails. He smacked his lips and licked his fingers. He leaned back and rubbed his belly.

"I know," she said as she put her hand on her ample hip. *You may be a little short but you can put away some food. Lord.* She finished putting the dishes in the dishwasher. Aja had already had her bath and was in her t-shirt and pajama bottoms watching television. "KJ's taking his bath, I'm gonna make sure he's not just sitting there. I know that trick!" She left Kevin at the kitchen table staring at the peach cobbler she had left cooling on top of the stove.

"Dang. She got me." Kevin shook his head. "No wonder Mr. Eastland stayed married so long. I'd stay too with food like this." He thought, Jewel *can do a little something but nothing like this.* He sucked the meat from the back of his tooth. By the time he'd finished a helping of peach cobbler and ice cream his mother-in-law had made sure all baths were done, school clothes were hung out, homework was done, and both kids were tucked in tight with no TV. "This camp is running like a well-oiled machine," Kevin muttered as he propped his feet up in the recliner.

The house was spotless, his belly was full, and the kids didn't utter a protest before getting in bed. No yelling, fighting, or tantrums. Mama Whitaker could stay for as long as she wanted as far as he was concerned. He stretched, then surfed the channels. He paused on T.D. Jakes. In seconds, his head had rolled back and he was dozing off. His mother-in-law came back downstairs and dropped on the couch.

"Now, see, this is why you can't have kids after a certain age. Too much work." She grabbed a magazine and fanned herself.

Kevin's eyes popped opened. "Huh, what? Man, I fell asleep." He watched as his mother-in-law reached down to rub her feet.

He smiled, then felt a little guilt tugging his spirit. "Mama Whitaker, you know I like having you here, it's just that…"

"Kevin, you don't have to say a word. Jewel meant well. I know my child better than anyone else. That thang is spoiled. The only reason I came is cause she bribed me with Shari's Berries and a cabin on the Tom Joyner cruise. You know Prince is coming? Besides, I really knew you could use the help. Kevin, I have never seen Jewel so committed to something. I knew when she went to law school that she was going for the wrong reasons. It was an expensive route but I think she finally found something she's passionate about and she's good at it!"

Kevin shook his head in agreement. "Yeah, she's a natural."

"Jewel needs our support." Mama Whitaker continued to fan. "Oooh, chile, I love me some Bishop Jakes but can we get a little Family Feud or Wendy Williams? You mind?"

"Naw, I don't mind. After Jewel and I had a little disagreement on the way to the airport, God spoke to me on the way home. He let me know what I really was tripping about. It's all this travel. I'ma be honest, I want her to succeed, but I don't think God wants her away from me and the kids so much to do it."

Mama Whitaker stared at Kevin's face. "If I were a betting woman, and I'm not," she said with the wisdom reflective of her silver tresses and parchment skin, "I'd think you're a little afraid, too."

"Of what?"

"Maybe she'll want something or someone else. Maybe she'll get out there and get all Hollywood and think this life's not good enough." She held out her hand. "Pay me my money."

"Naw," he said with knitted brows. "Maybe … not exactly."

"Listen to me, Kevin. Jewel loves you. God does not give us things to tear up family. Jewel's a lot more mature and wiser, and she's crazy about you and the kids. Trust the process. The worst thing you can do is clip a woman's wings. You've provided her a great life and paid off half her debt! I personally want to thank you for taking her off our hands!" Mama Whitaker cracked herself up at her last statement. "Seriously, what you've given Jewel goes beyond degrees or fancy cars. God's got this one. Something tells me this once opportunity may not be all it's cracked up to be." On that note, she winked. "I think I gonna turn in." She slowly rose off the couch, grabbing her back, then eased toward the stairs.

"Mama Whitaker," Kevin said when she hit the first step.

She paused without turning around, "You're welcome." She smiled and kept climbing the stairs.

Once he heard the guest bedroom door close, he turned the channel. After a few minutes of one of his favorite reality shows he lost interest and turned it off. He went upstairs, prayed then called his wife to say good night.

Chapter 32 – New Developments

Kevin turned on his computer, and before he had a chance to open Outlook, the phone rang.

"Eastland, can I see you in my office?" Wendell's voice was calm and measured.

Kevin sprang up, and without hesitation briskly walked to his boss' office. The door was already open.

Wendell waved him in. "Have a seat, close the door please."

Kevin sat down and clasped his hands in front of him. He focused on the large abstract painting that hung behind Wendell.

"So, what's going on?" he said, unable to decipher the reason for the visit from the stoic look of Wendell's face.

"First, just FYI, Heather no longer works here, so we'll be getting another admin. assistant soon."

"Oh, wow … she get a new job?" Kevin's eyes widened with curiosity.

"I'm really not at liberty to say." Wendell straightened his glasses with his hand. "I just needed to ask you a few questions and would appreciate your honest feedback." He leaned forward slightly and tapped the leather atop his desk with the end of a pencil.

"Did you know Heather really well?"

"Um, not really. Why do you ask?" Kevin responded, sensing the need to carefully choose his words.

"Just gathering some information, no worries. Did she ever mention having issues with anyone here on staff?"

"Issues? What kind of issues?" Kevin quizzed. "She okay? Something happened to her?" He braced himself for the response.

His face relaxed, "No, no…nothing like that. I think I'm going to let HR do their job. This is more for my personal information. If something affects my department I like do my research." Wendell jumped up and walked around his desk. "It's nothing really." He launched a crooked smile. "I'm just giving you the heads up … a few people have said they saw you after work one day in her car."

Kevin stood up. "I was helping her with her car situation. That's all."

"You can head back to your office. I'll keep you posted." He reached to shake Kevin's hand while he maintained eye contact.

Their hands moved in a mechanical fashion.

Once outside his door, Kevin uttered, "Father, I thank you that no weapon formed against me shall prosper." As he tried to make heads or tails of their conversation, his spirit churned. Despite a strong temptation to call Chad, he resisted. If anybody had the scoop, he did. But for now, a huge distraction in the form of work was calling him. Once at his desk, he focused on reviewing his budget and responding to e-mail. He decided to leave any investigative work to God, and mind his own business.

~~~~~

Despite a morning that left him a bit unsettled, Kevin managed to get a lot done. He was about to break for a light lunch when his cellphone went off. "Hmm," he thought as *The Gifted Academy* scrolled across the screen. "Hope Aja's not sick."

"Mr. Eastland?"

"Yes, this is he."

"I'm Esther Evans, the Assistant Principal here at your daughter's school. I was calling to let you know we had a little incident."

"What type of incident? Aja never gets in any trouble."

"I know sir. It's a little complicated. That's why I didn't want to have to make this call."

"So what happened, what's going on?"

"Calm down. She isn't hurt or in trouble. But it would probably be a good idea if you came down here. She said your wife was out of town. We were going to have her grandmother come but she isn't listed on file."

"Okay, but I need to know what's going on," he said, his heart pulsating.

The principal hesitated.

"Please, just tell him to come here," Aja whined.

"Sir, I think it probably would be better to talk in person."

"Okay, I'm coming right now." He grabbed his keys. "Ma'am, I'll get there as soon as I can." He made a quick call to his boss, letting him know he had a bit of an emergency. Wendell was fine with him taking off early. At the least, Wendell was a family man who was empathetic to family issues.

~~~~~

When Kevin walked into the assistant principal's office, his daughter was seated in a chair with her head down. As soon as she saw her father she ran over and hugged him. She sobbed, "Take me home."

"What's wrong?" He rubbed her hair then looked at the assistant principal with a curious expression.

The tall black woman with short honey blond hair mouthed, "She got 'her friend' today."

Kevin froze and his forehead creased. "Friend. What's her name?"

She frowned and shook her head, "No, her *friend*."

"Oh, oh!" He stuttered, "No! What? How?" *She's just a baby. My baby. Oh Jesus. Of all times for Jewel to be out of town.* He tried to be calm and not reflect the panic he felt on the inside, but he was gonna get Aja to her grandmother ASAP!

Chapter 33 - Preaching on the Plane

Jewel thought she'd died and gone to private jet heaven. When the driver pulled up to Van Nuys airport, she held her breath then exhaled. *God, this was so on my vision board! You are the bomb!* Minutes later, she was seated on the five-passenger jet next to McKenzie. *My sleek high ponytail was the perfect choice for the jet set!*

Once in the air, they immediately ran through the week's agenda. "So, I found three wineries for potential wedding venues," McKenzie said as she peeked over at Jewel's planning notes. "Meadowwood, which is gorgeous and modern; The Churchill Manor, and the Villagio Inn and Day Spa."

Jewel was quickly searching websites on her I-Pad for visuals. "The Meadowood is gorgeous and the Villagio has just a hint of rustic elegance, but it's classy. What did your groom say?"

McKenzie flipped her long layered hair behind one shoulder and brushed a finger beneath her enhanced eyelash. "He only wants the best." Her throat seemed to become instantly dry, and she coughed. "How about some champagne?"

"Before noon? I'll pass. So, have you thought about your bridesmaids?" Jewel continued to flip through the website galleries.

"I'm a little torn. Of course, my sister Natalie will be my matron of honor. She'll be the only immediate family. She's catty, jealous, may ruin my day but I feel obligated. My mother and I are barely speaking." McKenzie wanted to take back the words as quickly as they rolled off her lips.

"Not speaking, why? We've got to have the MOB."

"MOB?" McKenzie's face cinched.

"Mother of the Bride," Jewel clarified.

"Oh. Well, for one, she hates that I'm in L.A. After college, she wanted me to come back to Mudpie, Mississippi to work in the church. The last time we spoke was at my Dad's funeral. And if I don't have the wedding at the church, she surely won't come." She sighed. "The way I see it, everything God made *is* the church."

Wow, that's a lot, but God, she's got a point on the church thing.

"The truth? I think my own mother's jealous of me."

McKenzie took a deep breath. "I mean, it was hard, but I took some big risks and I carved my own path," she said, almost trying to convince herself. "I have my own life to live. That's why I haven't gone back in years. Too much negative energy. If you breathed wrong…it was a sin–wearing pants, jewelry, make-up, playing music in church, *all wrong*. When I got to college I was so naïve. I felt like a freak!"

"That's really deep," Jewel empathized. "I don't know, maybe your parents were a little extreme but they probably had your best interest at heart. But for them, you may never have had a relationship with God. And to know Him from such a young age is worth so much. Back in college, I never understood why you sang and prayed so much, but I do now. I apologize if I ever made you feel weird because of it. It was my ignorance. As believers, it's up to us to stand up and stand out, despite criticism. We have to be the light of this world." She took a deep breath. *Whoa, did I just say that? Preach Jewel!*

"Now you sound like my mother. It's easier said than done. All I know is I had to be free from all those rules. Religion was suffocating me. Look, can we talk about something else? Like, umm, the bridesmaids. Now, I've been going back and forth between Jewel's Rule #22 –Never let the bridesmaids outshine the bride or the 'Optics Rule'.

Jewel cringed. *I said that?* "So what's the 'Optics Rule'?"

"Oh, always hang around photogenic people, especially at major events. It's a L.A. thing. I mean, let's be realistic, you can't Photoshop *everything*. Sooo, with that in mind, Natalie's a go, and for bridesmaids: Avery Ashton, a striking interior designer and Ariane Michaels a socialite and heir to a soft drink dynasty. I think we have the winners, a wedding party certain to appeal to the right press!" McKenzie leaned back as if she'd accomplished some major feat.

Jewel's mouth twisted. She put her I-Pad down. "Sweetie…about Jewel's Rules–that was like a long time ago, and certainly not meant to be followed verbatim. There's room for flexibility."

"I know, but Jewel, you've always had such wisdom. And you always managed to get exactly what you wanted. You walk in any room and capture attention. That's why when I have to make decisions, I still ask myself, "Would this be 'Jewel Approved?' It could be an outfit, restaurant, or a career move…"

Jewel teetered between telling her friend that she had no clue about what she was doing back then and basking in her rays of adoration. So she tried a compromise. "McKenzie. You are your own brand of fabulousness now. Some of Jewel's Rules are relevant, but you have to search deep in your heart for what's true to you. On your wedding day, you want to be surrounded by the people who love and support you most, regardless of some silly optics." She grabbed her arm, "Besides, we can make anybody look good!"

"Yeah, but I'm still going with my picks to be safe. I know it's what Horace would want."

Jewel raised her infamous church finger. "Right, you know I'm going to the bathroom. I've been holding it." She walked a few feet and lunged into the bathroom. She took deep breaths, and fanned herself with her hand, "God, please forgive me. I think I have singlehandedly messed her and an entire population of women up." She grabbed a paper towel and ran cool water over it, then pressed it against her neck. "She's got a major obsession with *moi* and a case of approval addiction. Lord I get it. This isn't just a

job or a check…it's an assignment!"

Chapter 34 – Back in H-Town on the Ground

"She's a model. Well, she used to be a model for some relaxer box back in the day. Fabulaxer or something like that," Jermane said as she paced her husband's law office. "And he wants us all to go to mass on Easter Sunday then have brunch." She pressed her hand against her forehead.

"Baby, read this memo," her husband, Rex, grabbed the paper from the printer and handed it to her.

"Are you listening to me?" Jermane dropped into Rex's leather wingback chair.

He took a deep breath. "Sweetie, your father's had plenty of lady friends before. What is it about this one that's bugging you?" He clasped his hands and studied her face.

Jermane popped out of the chair, "Albany...her name's Albany. Ugh!" She rolled her eyes. "Anyway she's forty five, he's sixty-eight. That's like twenty-three years apart. Hello? Golddigger." She threw her arms up and allowed them to fall alongside her tan pencil skirt. "And, get this. I think he mentioned marriage, at his age? C'mon." Her hand fumbled with her pearl necklace.

"I don't see anything wrong with it. Baby, let the man be happy. Why don't you spend a little time with the woman. "He's your father but he's also a man, with needs."

"Please, spare me." She quipped. "I really don't want to talk about that." She bit the side of her thumb and tapped her foot. "She's a gold digger. I just know it. I mean my Dad's handsome and charming but feels like gold digger is written all over this."

Oh brother. "Not everybody who dates your Dad wants money." Rex got up and placed his arms around Jermane. "Honey, you have been a Daddy's girl all your life and you always will be. You're father has an iron clad will, he's smart and has all his faculties. Stop worrying." He kissed the side of her neck and she closed her eyes.

"Mmm. You always know what to do to calm my nerves. But I'm mad you're taking his side."

"I'm not on anybody's side. And if your husband can't soothe you, who can?" he whispered. He smiled roguishly as he walked to the door and locked it. "I'm thinking, since you came all the way over here to see me, I deserve some undivided attention, especially since you are looking too good in that skirt." His eyes ranged freely up and down his wife's body. He sat on the desk and pulled her toward him.

She flashed a sheepish grin as she wrapped her arms around his neck. Before she could utter another word, he kissed her in a way that would surely make her forget all her cares. Hot waves swept through her just like the first time they'd locked eyes in law school. And for the moment the issue of her father and his girlfriend were placed on hold for more important "business".

Chapter 35 – Get Ready

Angel wrapped up a small box of Octavio's personal items. In anticipation of her faith move, she committed to a cleaning project each week. Her massive shelves of collected books were the current goal. As hard as it was, she was able to part with a large amount deciding only to keep her favorites and autographed copies. *Off to Half Price Books on Saturday.*

She closed and labeled the last box. *D.C. or bust.* She stood up and took in the chic décor of her spacious, two-story condo, pondering whether to sell or keep it as a rental property. *Still praying on that.* Seconds later, the phone rang. When she saw the number, her smile turned downward.

"Hey, Aunt Dot. How are you? Everything okay?"

"Well, it could be better. Your Uncle Frank's got Gout and your cousin Tootie is back on that stuff."

Angel sighed inwardly and rolled her eyes. "I'm sorry to hear that, Auntie."

"Well, you know how it goes. But I won't complain."

You just did. She imagined her Aunt in one of her colorful Mumus, with her silver dreadlocks grazing her shoulders. "So, now sweetie, I know you're trying, but I'm not going to be able to look out for your mother much longer. She's getting down right mean. And she fell the other day. It's a lot on me."

"I know Aunt Dot, and I really do appreciate it." Angel fell back on her chaise lounge and stared at the ceiling as her aunt rambled on about the CIA listening in on their phone.

"Sweetie, you should have come home a long time ago. You need this time with your mother. Each day she gets a little worse. The other day she wanted me to help her get dressed. She thought her students were waiting, like she was a professor back at Howard. Poor thing, really hurt my heart."

Angel put the phone on speaker. She knew her aunt would be going on for a while. It's not that she didn't want to hear it, okay, she really didn't want to hear it. To her own admission, Angel was a bit in denial.

"Angel, baby," her aunt croaked, "You there?"

"Yeah, yes, Aunt Dot. I'm working on it. I think I may have a job lined up. I'm just waiting on confirmation."

"Well, I wouldn't wait too long. That big house is paid for, so at least you won't have to find a place to live. That's half the battle." Her aunt sighed. "Anyway, I need to get off this phone. Seems like nobody else does anything around here accept me. I'm getting old, too."

She knew her aunt meant well, but her voice brought stabs of anxiety and dread to Angel's spirit. "Aunt Dot, I don't mean to rush off but I got to um, um…put the trash out."

"You said you're going out. Oh, okay sweetie. Call me later."

Her aunt never said goodbye, she'd just hang up whether she was in the middle of a thought or not. Angel felt drained from her cleaning project and speaking with her aunt. So, she spent the next hour or so doing yoga and meditation. She took a short but very soothing soak in the tub and threw on some comfy clothes. She was about to pick up her Bible to read, when Lexi called. "Wow, this is a nice surprise. What's up?"

"Girl, gotta get in chat time when I can. You were on my mind. Little Chris is asleep, so I can talk without a gazillion interruptions. Have you been getting some of Jewel's Instagrams?" Lexi started loading her dishwasher.

"Need you need to ask?" They both laughed.

"I think our girl has finally arrived," Lexi added.

"You know I'm proud of her, she's come a long way." Angel dropped on the couch.

"Yeah she has. We all have really."

"Sooo, no word on the job?" Lexi put a plate in the microwave for Chris.

"Not yet. But I know it's coming. God spoke the word loud and clear, '*You will relocate to D.C. for a job.*' A few hours after He spoke, I get a call from one of my mentors, telling me to apply for this position. So, I have to be patient. When God has orders our steps, we don't need to look for an elevator. I'm just trying to be ready."

"I hear you, sis. Sooo, are you absolutely certain He told you and Octavio to call it quits? I'm going to miss you two together. Every time I hear that song *All of Me* by John Legend I think of Angel and Octavio, the early years!" She laughed.

I knew this was coming. "I'm sure, Lex. If I missed it, God will let me know. I wish all you hopeless romantics accepted the fact that marriage isn't for everybody. Octavio wants marriage and kids, and I think it's selfish to keep him from having that. He comes from a huge Latin family. He may be okay now but I don't want him to resent me later.

Do I miss him? Yes. Do I still think about him? Of course. He was such a huge part of my life. But, right about now, I'm so head over heels in love with Jesus it doesn't matter." She got up and went to the bathroom. She looked under her medicine cabinet to get her comb and hair moisturizer to start twisting her hair.

"I know that feeling. I admire your confidence in the season you're in. We're always rushing to get to something. When we're single, we rush to get married. When we're married we rush to get the house, kids and the dream job. I think for now I'm just gonna try to enjoy the moment. Trust me, marriage is a huge commitment. And a kid? A twenty-four hour job my sister." Lexi took a deep breath.

"But Lexi, you seem like such a natural," Angel said with a faint smile. On the way back to the living room, she turned on the I-pod and allowed Jill Scott's version of *Lovely Day* to fill the living room. She was relaxed again.

"Yeah…wouldn't trade my son for the world. But we truly need to be ready for whatever we ask God for and open to the way it comes. Trouble doesn't give you a pass once you're married with a kid. Matter of fact, God ups the ante on the prayer needs. I get up earlier, work harder, and pray twice as hard. It's quite a work-out."

"But you make it look so easy." Angel put the phone on speaker and started parting and twisting her hair into two strands.

"Really? I always feel like I'm rushing around holding everything together with a safety pin. I find myself yelling and fussing at the both of them. I've been getting frustrated so easily."

"Yeah, me too, but I think I may be a little perimenopausal. I blame it all on that." Angel laughed.

"Ugh, I *hate* that word. It just sounds old." Lexi sat down and pulled her laundry basket toward her. "Girl, we're still young and fine. I haven't even hit forty yet."

"Yeah, but it's a reality. Since I'll get to that neighborhood before you, I'll let you know about the magic ride." Angel laughed. "You got time."

"As long as you don't start yelling 'I'm flashin' every five minutes in public, like some crazed woman. Uh, who needs to know all that?"

Angel laughed then grew quiet. "Lex, I know I can tell you anything." She took a deep breath, "There's something that I haven't shared with the girls."

"What's going on?" She continued to fold her clothes. "Sounds serious."

"Um, yeah. Wasn't holding out on purpose. Sometimes I have to process things first."

"What's going on, sis?" Lexi paused during folding a shirt.

"Well, maybe I'm in a wee bit of denial." She took a deep breath and placed the comb on the couch. "It's my mom. She's been diagnosed with early Dementia."

"Oh, Angel. I'm so sorry." Lexi closed her eyes for a minute then opened them.

"I feel this major guilt because I really haven't been there. My aunt's been taking care of her but I need to go home. It's pretty bitter-sweet."

"Wow, yeah, that's rough. So why *haven't* you gone home more often?"

"It was all about my Ex. He could do no wrong. His mother and my mother were best friends. We grew up together. I don't know, he was far from what he portrayed himself to be. They really didn't know him. And Lex, I need to come clean about something else…" Angel bit her lip before she spoke.

"Okay…"

"I wasn't really divorced *because* I was never actually married." She took a deep breath. "I sort of left him at the altar."

Chapter 36 – Tulle Rules

"Aren't you excited? You finally locked down a venue. I think moving the date forward was good. Now we're full steam ahead," Jewel said. "Their Events Director seems fabulous. I mean she's already taking care of flowers, tents, and a ton of things I can cross off my 'to do' list." Jewel said as they walked into the Lili Bridal Shop.

"Yes, it's beautiful. The view, simply breathtaking, and I could just picture the wedding. I love the idea of the hot air balloon rides, and the pictures will be gorgeous!" They were greeted by a staff member and before they knew it McKenzie was whisked away to a fitting area.

"So, McKenzie, let me see the first dress," Jewel said as she awaited the bride to be.

McKenzie was an absolute vision in a strapless form fitting fit and flare. "That's gorgeous, satin is dreamy," Jewel gasped.

McKenzie turned and inspected her back side. "I love this. I mean I absolutely love it. I never expected to find a dress today.

I just wanted to get an idea." She pulled her long hair to one side as the consultant stepped back in admiration. "It's like a perfect fit." Her smile instantly faded. "I don't know. I just want to try a few more."

McKenzie tried on dresses for the next two hours. She exhausted the consultant, Jewel, and all the managers. They pulled just about every dress and style. "You know, I just think I really can't make a final decision until I actually visit the Vera Wang store. That's always been my dream," she said matter-of-factly.

Jewel was seething. *I know this chick does not want to fly to New York.* Just when Jewel was about to tell her about herself, she thought about that big fat check at the end of the wedding rainbow and she took a deep breath. Before she knew it, McKenzie was standing in front of the three-way mirror balling her eyes out.

Jewel shot up and walked over. "McKenzie, what's wrong?"

McKenzie sobbed continuously for about ten minutes. The bridal consultant handed her a box of tissue and she went through half of it. She sat on a bench and finally took a deep breath, her face swollen from crying. "I'm so sorry. I just, um. I think," she weighed her words carefully, "I just need my mom," she whispered.

"Hey, hey there's absolutely nothing wrong with that," Jewel said as she gave her friend a hug and wiped her eyes. "Guess what? She's just a phone call away. I bet she's been wanting to talk to you, just as much as you've needed her."

McKenzie looked up with hope-filled eyes, "Think so?"

"Yeah. Why don't we take a little break? Say a little prayer and give her a call. We can invite the bridesmaids and have a mini-brunch so we all can celebrate you."

She shook her head as she dabbed her eyes. "Sounds good."

Chapter 37 – Baby Girl

Jewel breathed a sigh of relief when she made it back to Houston Saturday morning. She was also grateful that Kevin had been there waiting for her as soon as she came out of the baggage area. However, he was unusually quiet on the way home. She had an entire day to rest, and just as she suspected, her house was spotless and all seemed perfect in the Eastland household.

Shortly after she walked through the door, KJ came running into the living room, yelling, "Mommy!!!"

She grabbed and hugged him, planting kisses all over his face, which he promptly wiped away. "Okay Mommy okay!" he said, smacking on a piece of gum.

"Where's Aja?" Jewel said, expecting her daughter to come running down the steps as well.

"Huh?" Kevin shoved his hands in his pockets. "Baby, all I'm going to say is I listened to your mother and I was going to call you right away but I didn't want you to worry. We handled it." He rocked back on his heels and smiled.

"Handled what?" Jewel sneered.

By this time her mother came into the living room. "Hey sweetie, how was your trip? You look so rested. You hungry? I cooked your favorite."

"Okay, that's it. Something happened. What is it?"

"Well, I didn't want you to worry but Aja got her period while you were gone."

Jewel felt her heart drop. "Aja? My baby Aja? Omigod! Is she okay?"

Her mother shook her head. "She's fine. Just a little embarrassed, but fine."

Jewel went and sat on the couch. "She's just a baby."

"It happens. It's that processed food kids eat today. They are starting sooner." Her mother looked at Kevin.

"I just wish you all would have called me." She looked back and forth at the two of them. "I could have talked to her," Jewel said quietly as she shook her head. "I mean, I'm the only mother she has." She was more shocked than angry. Her first intuition was to run upstairs, tear into Aja's room and hug her. But for some reason she was paralyzed.

They all stood there silent for a few minutes until her mother finally broke the silence, "Okay, she got her period, she's not pregnant. It's normal. Now, can we eat so I can finally get home to my husband?"

Chapter 38 – Back up Bestie

Jewel tried to take a nap but something was eating her up. She didn't make it a habit, but from time to time she opted to stay home from church. She watched a little Joyce Meyer then closed her eyes. No matter how hard she tried, her soul would not rest. She thought about McKenzie, and although she was a little upset at her mother she could not imagine not talking to her at least once a week. She finally dozed off and woke up two hours later to find the house empty. She figured Kevin probably took the kids to get something to eat so she could get a little more rest. She rolled over and picked up the phone to call Lexi.

"Hey girl," Jewel said.

"Hey sis, little Chris …you're gonna get a whipping if you don't sit down! Sorry girl, we stopped at Chuckie Cheese after church. Lord why! Chris, are you watching him!" she yelled.

Jewel needed to talk and she needed Lexi's full attention. She wasn't trying to be selfish but it was difficult with little Chris clowning in the background. "Lexi, look girl I'll call you back. Spend time with the family."

She rolled over on her side and dialed another one of her girls, "Hey Angel."

"Jewel?" *She never calls me, Lexi must be busy.*

"Yeah, girl it's me. I just had some things on my mind and needed to talk."

"What's up?" she said as she laced up her tennis shoes.

"Mmm, I don't know."

"Oh, hold that thought. Jermane told me to tell you that Easter Brunch is at her house this year. Catered. She's having an Easter egg hunt; Capri and Anthony are bringing the kids from his charity, blah, blah. Just be there and bring your kids."

"Nobody told me. I always do the holidays."

"I just did. Jewel, be thankful. You get a break. She said something about her dad bringing his new girlfriend. She needed some back up."

Jewel rolled her eyes. "Okay, whatever. I just wanted your opinion about something."

"My opinion. The illustrious Jewel Whitaker wants MY opinion."

"Angel, please this is serious."

"Okay, okay," she said as she stood and bounced on her toes.

"You know how you pray for something and you get it, and you're still not happy?"

"Yep, that's cause we make the mistake of thinking 'things' are going to make us happy."

"I guess."

"What is it Jewel? Spit it out." Angel filled her water bottle.

"Okay, Aja started her cycle and nobody called me! I mean that was a monumental event, and… well, a girl needs her mother. She's so young. I had a long talk with her when I got back, but don't you think Kevin or my mother should have told me?"

"Jewel, they probably didn't want you to panic. They know how much this client means and Lexi just thought–" *Oops.*

"Lexi? Lexi told Kevin not to tell me? How many other people knew before I did?" Jewel jumped off the bed.

"Jewel, calm down. I guess Kevin panicked. He called Lexi on the way back from picking Aja up and we were grabbing a late lunch. "Please, Jewel, don't make a big deal out of it."

click

Crap!

Chapter 39 – Easter Brunch

Jermane put the finishing touches on the formal dining table. She rarely used her linen and silverware but thought this was the perfect occasion. She'd ordered several flower arrangements to make the place look festive. After the brunch, they'd start the Easter egg hunt. Anthony was going to pick up several kids from his charity to participate. Her father hadn't arrived, but she was going to do her best to make her Dad and his girlfriend feel comfortable. Even if she had to pray the whole time.

Rex walked into the living room and kissed her on the cheek. "Looks beautiful, babe."

Jermane turned around and hugged him. "Thanks, but you know I can't all take the credit. The caterers." She smiled.

Several minutes later Lexi, Chris, and her son, Angel and the rest of the invited guests filed in. The table was a beautiful spread of several meats, side dishes, garden fresh vegetables, homemade bread, salad, a custom punch and desserts. Before they were seated for dinner Rex said the prayer.

As soon as the prayer ended, Jermane heard the clang of forks against the plates and very little talking, at first.

"So, play-offs are looking good, my man. Thanks for keeping us in the house," Kevin said.

"Yeah, looks like we're in this thing to win it this year," Anthony raised his glass.

"Oh, so we were thinking, everybody could come to the next game here in Houston. Anthony can take care of the seats," Capri added as she adjusted the napkin on her lap.

"You ain't said but a word," Kevin chomped on his greens.

"Baby, can you finish chewing your food before you talk?" Jewel quipped.

Kevin didn't respond as his eyes fell to his plate.

Rex cleared his throat. "So, how's that job coming? Proud of you man."

"Thanks, Rex man. Going good, I'm learning a lot. And I'm finally about to finish up that business degree. Can't wait to finish up school. Got two more courses."

"Well, let us know when the graduation ceremony is … we'll all be there."

Soon, Jermane's father Avery Jacobs walked through the door hand in hand with his girlfriend, Albany.

"There's your new stepmother," Capri whispered, then laughed.

Jermane kicked her under the table.

Rex stood up and shook his father-in-law's hand. "Hey Dad."

"Hey, son, this is Albany Rand." He said proudly.

Rex shook her hand. "Nice to meet you."

"Likewise," she said quietly, as she held tight to Jermane's father. She was tall, fit and her cocoa brown skin glowed. Her shoulder length hair was styled in loose waves and parted in the middle.

"She's pretty," Lexi whispered.

"Golddigger," Jermane uttered.

"And this is my one and only beautiful daughter." Her father spoke as they made their way around the table toward their seats.

Jermane was hesitant but stood. "Hi," Jermane said, void of any emotion. "Welcome to our home." Her voice was lifeless and monotone.

Albany reached out for a hug.

"Smile," Lexi said through clenched teeth.

Jermane gave Albany an obligatory church hug. "Please have a seat," Jermane said as she pointed toward the empty chairs.

~~~~

Once the food and wine began to flow, the conversation livened up. "So we were just talking about getting together for the next game. Anthony plays for the Houston Meteors," Chris said.

"Oh, I know. I'm a huge fan," Albany said. "I love sports."

Jermane leaned over to Lexi. "See what I mean?"

"Soo, Albany, you used to model, I can see that?" Kevin asked.

Jewel cut her eyes. "What do you mean you could see that?"

"I mean she's tall, you know and attractive. She just has that look…"

"Eh-em. Yes, I used to model, but that was a long time ago. My second career was a nurse. I've done a lot of private duty."

"I bet," Jermane said as she sipped her wine.

"Okay, sweetie that's enough wine for you." Rex grabbed her glass as she made eye contact with her father. He looked very disappointed.

"So, how about we get those eggs together," Lexi said as she slid away from the table. "Those kids from the charity will be here in about an hour."

"Good idea," Capri said as she shot up from the table.

"Yeah. I'll help," Angel said as she rushed to the kitchen and yanked Jermane's arm.

~~~~

"Okay, Jermane, knock it off," Angel demanded as they reached the kitchen.

"What? I think I'm being cordial." She added several colored eggs to the baskets.

"No you're not," Lexi warned. "You're being ugly."

"I'm telling you. I know she's using my Dad. He's been trouncing all over the country. Golfing, Zip Lining, camping. He is too old for that. It's not safe."

"I think that's great. He needs to be active," Capri added.

"Jermane, just give her a chance."

"If I wanted your opinions I'd ask." Jermane threw open the fridge and grabbed more eggs. The doorbell rang and she marched to get it. She opened the door. "The Easter Bunny is here!" she yelled in a voice void of any joy. She waved him to the back yard.

~~~~

Once the eggs were hidden, the kids from Anthony's charity showed up. They went crazy in the large garden searching for eggs. Anthony was having as much fun as the kids. Capri watched him the whole time. His smile was big, he laughed, wrestled, and he gave them hugs.

"That man's a natural with kids," Lexi said as she noticed Capri staring out the window. She brought in several empty baskets and set them on the table.

"Yeah," Capri unfolded her arms and sat down.

"So, you sure you don't want any kids?"

"Umm, we'll see." Capri gave Lexi a sly look.

"Welp, it won't happen if you don't try," Lexi said.

"Who says we're not trying?" Capri flashed a huge grin and winked her eye.

~~~~~

Jermane walked her Dad and his date to the front door. Most everyone had left except Jewel, who was waiting on Kevin. He was still running his mouth with Rex and she was growing impatient.

"Albany, do you mind? I'll meet you in the car," Jermane's dad said.

"Okay," she said. "Jermane, it was so nice meeting you." She eased out the door way.

Jermane's father started right in. "Jermane, you are my pride and joy. But the way you behaved towards Albany was inexcusable. You were so rude."

"Dad, I was not." Her wine had worn off.

"Now, I don't know what your problem is, but Albany is a genuine and sincere person. She makes me happy and I happen to be in love with her."

Jermane's eyes grew wide.

"And I have asked her to marry me. We're getting married in two weeks."

"What! Are you getting a prenup?"

"If I chose to get a prenup it's none of your business" He was about to turn and walk out.

"She's a golddigger!" Jermane shouted.

"You have *no* proof of that. You don't even know her. You don't want to know her. She didn't want to come here. But I assured her that you would at least be courteous and make an effort. Surely I thought Jermane, my daughter whom I love more than anything, would at least treat her decent and make her feel welcome. Well, I was wrong!"

Jermane had never heard her father yell like that.
"Dad, you don't know these women today. Trust me, I know a golddigger when I see one, I've been friends with one for years!"

Jewel had just walked in the living room. She stood behind Jermane, electrocuted and stunned by her words. She slowly walked up and faced her. "So, that's what you think of me?"

"Jewel, no I didn't mean it like that. I'm sorry. You're not like that anymore. I mean you said yourself..."

"Kevin," Jewel yelled. "Kevin!"

He rushed to the front of the house.

"Get the kids, let's go."

"What, what happened?"

"Get the kids, let's go! Now."

"Okay, alright." He turned around gathered Aja and little Kevin and they all rushed out the door without an explanation.

Jermane's father looked at his daughter and shook his head. "I hope you're satisfied. Happy Easter."

Chapter 40 – My Soft Place the Land

"What happened?" Kevin quizzed as they drove away.

"I don't want to talk about it right now." Jewel turned up the radio.

"It must have been pretty bad for you to storm out like that. You and Jermane never argue."

"Well, you think you know people," Jewel mumbled.

"What do you mean by that?" Kevin glanced sideways but kept his voice down since the kids were asleep in the back seat.

"Nothing," she said with a voice as cold as death.

"Jewel, something's wrong. If you don't communicate I won't know what's wrong." He focused on the road.

"Okay, why did you go to Lexi about Aja before you told me? I'm your wife.

You don't get advice from my friends about things that concern our children."

"Jewel," he said quietly. "I didn't mean to disrespect you. You were out of town I panicked. If I would have told you, you would have jumped back on that plane and come back home."

She turned to Kevin, "Yes, I probably would have."

"Jewel, it's water under the bridge. Aja's fine," he said in a low voice.

"Kevin, before I left, Aja was up under me the entire night. She kept talking about me not leaving her and how she needed a mom. I don't know. I guess it messed me up that I couldn't be here. I feel like I mess up everything. What made me think I could be a wife and mother?" She sighed.

"Now if you talk like that, I'm going to have to pull over and…I don't know, kiss you."

Jewel sighed and smiled a bit. "I don't know what I'm gonna do with you."

"Now, I want you to stop putting all this pressure on yourself. I want you to concentrate on this job. Do you think the enemy is just going to let you walk through this season of blessing without stirring up a little drama? You need to brush off all this doubt and worry."

"Now you can pull over," she commanded.

"Why? Something wrong?" he said.

"Nothing, just wanted to give my husband a kiss."

Without another word, he obliged his wife's request. "You ain't said nothing but a word!" He pulled over on a neighborhood street.

"Why are we stopping?" Aja said, half asleep.

They both leaned over and their lips met.

"Oh God," Aja said, then fell back.

"I'm grateful," Jewel said. "You're my soft place to land and I thank God for it. I don't know anyone more patient and forgiving than you."

"Yeah baby because YOU, you're a handful and you require a lot."

Chapter 41 – Schoolin' Life

Jermane packed up her outlines and materials. She'd just closed her lecture on the Statute of Frauds. It was an area of contracts that seemed so simple, but one in which she struggled. She had her Dad to thank for finally getting her to understand what falling "within and outside the Statute of Frauds" meant. He was there when she had that "aha moment". As a matter of fact, he was always there. He was there when she filled out all her law school applications. There for her cotillion. There for her wedding, there the day she got sworn in to the State Bar of Texas. Jermane took a deep breath and a wave of guilt swept over her. She still had not spoken to her father since Easter.

I don't know what came over me. God, whatever caused me to act that way, please change it. She looked out into the empty seats of the lecture hall, remembering her first week of law school. She had been terrified, not knowing what to expect. "Look to your left, look to your right, one of you won't be here." But she and all her girls made it. They'd decided right then and there that it was all or nothing. "No lawyer left behind." She took a deep breath and smiled at the thought.

That week was also the first time she met Rex. From the first words they spoke, she knew he was the one. They were inseparable. She'd always wondered why God blessed her so easily with a husband, while other women seemingly struggled to meet the one. Although God never made it clear, she thought maybe he owed her since she'd lost her mother at such a young age.

Jermane remembered when her father first met Rex. That day, he said, "I just met my future law partner and son-in-law." Rex was so honored and her father was so proud. He knew right away the kind of man Rex was. She paused, removed her glasses and put her head down to mumble a quick prayer.

Father I don't know why I behaved the way I did. Forgive me. I just pray that You help me to put away my selfishness and be open to whatever blessings You want to bring my father's way. I guess I am spoiled but I have never disrespected my father. And I also pray that Jewel and Albany will find it in their hearts to forgive me.

When Jermane raised her head, she felt a huge weight lift from her. She had this extreme sense of peace. She got up from the chair, grabbed her briefcase, and headed toward the door. The Dean's secretary rushed around the corner just as she stepped out.

"Professor Richmond!" she said, sounding a little winded. Her legs were short and stocky, so moving fast was a bit of a labor. "Your husband, Attorney Richmond, has been trying to reach you for the last few minutes. He said for you to call him right now."

"Oh, okay, did he say what he wanted?" She pulled her phone out of her purse and looked down. He'd tried to call her five times. She dialed right away, without waiting for the Dean's secretary to answer.

"I need to run back to the office. I left the front desk unattended."

"Baby, what's going on … everything okay?" she said after connecting with Rex.

"Hey, I've been trying to call you."

"You know I turn my ringer off during the lecture. You sound out of breath, where are you? " Her forehead creased.

She heard footsteps, and in seconds, he was at the doorway. "I'm here."

She stared at him curiously. "Rex, tell me what's wrong."

"When you didn't answer your phone, I decided to drive right over. It's, it's your Dad, sweetie." He paused. "He ... um ... they were on the golf course and he had this intense pain. They rushed him to the hospital."

Jermane saw Rex's mouth move, but heard no sound after the word 'hospital'. "So, what are you saying, babe?" Her words were calm and measured as she searched his eyes.

"Baby, he had an aneurism and died before they reached the hospital. I'm so, I'm so sorry."

She looked at him as if he were speaking a foreign language. She walked slowly toward him and shook her head. "No, no, not my Dad."

Rex rushed over to Jermane and grabbed her just as her legs gave way. "Aw baby, aw sweetie, I'm so sorry. So sorry." Her tears flowed as he wrapped her tight against his chest. "Shh, I'm here. I'm here," he said as he rocked her.

Chapter 42 – Yes to the Dress?

"Me and my big mouth." Jewel found herself flying the friendly skies again, but this time her destination was New York ... for McKenzie's first official bride gown search at Vera Wang. McKenzie had followed Jewel's advice and called her mother. As Jewel predicted, her mother was overjoyed to hear her daughter's voice. Much of her mother's beliefs had been tied to her husband and when he died so did some of the "religion" that kept them both bound. Quite naturally, McKenzie flew her mother out to join them.

Despite the fact that Jewel was not speaking to Jermane and was still a little ticked at Lexi, she would have rather been at home. Especially since her son had cried and held her leg for about fifteen minutes before she walked out the door. So, her flight to LaGuardia was far from restful, but rather consumed with guilt that could not even be soothed by a fabulous room at the Waldorf.

Jewel picked up the phone to see what time they all needed to meet downstairs. She purposefully avoided meeting

McKenzie's mother. She pictured a big haired bible toting,

country bumpkin wearing a two-piece powder blue suit and zero

sense of style. *This ought to be fun.* McKenzie answered the

phone, and Jewel said, "Hello my gorgeous bride to be!" *Cue the*

acting skills. "Are we ready to find our dream dress?"

"Oh, I'm so looking forward to this! Mama is too,"

McKenzie said. "Be downstairs in about fifteen minutes, the car is

on its way."

"With bells on!" Jewel sang and rolled her eyes.

~~~~~

Jewel exited the elevator and noticed McKenzie in a black

and white dress standing by the Concierge. She threw up her hand.

"Hey, sweetie. You look beautiful as always." They air kissed.

"Oh, Mom!"

A woman came up behind Jewel from the direction of the

restroom. "Oh, you must be the infamous Jewel! So nice to meet

you dear! I heard so much about you and you are as pretty as you

want to be!" She grabbed and hugged Jewel.

Jewel was stunned. McKenzie's mother was elegant and

poised. She looked every bit the MOB part in a black sheath dress, a chic bob, and a bold statement necklace. "So nice to meet you," Jewel said, stopping short of actually saying, "You're nothing like I imagined." McKenzie's mother even wore make up. "So we are off to Vera's," Jewel announced.

~~~~~

When they arrived at the dress shop, they were escorted to a private dressing area. Jewel met with the consultant who pulled several selections. After trying on about five dresses, McKenzie had it narrowed down to a gorgeous fit and flare from Vera Wang's classics collection named "Fiona". She stood and turned in the mirror as she ran her hand over the architectural and modern strapless top and the beautiful tiered bottom. "This is just so gorgeous."

"Okay, just for fun, why don't you try on this? I just have a hunch." The bridal consultant handed McKenzie a strapless gown called "Helena".

All Jewel saw was chiffon, lace, and a light layering of ruffles. *I don't know how this is gonna go down*, she thought. But when McKenzie walked out wearing that gown, she looked as if she were walking on air. She looked so ethereal. Her mother was at a loss for word. McKenzie looked in the mirror and did a turn.

"So?" Jewel said.

McKenzie didn't say a word, but the tears fell.

She has her dress, she had her moment. I get to go home. Yes!

~~~~~

"I am in love with my dress!" McKenzie shouted as they got in the car. "It's the most gorgeous thing ever."

"That is one beautiful dress," her mother said. "Well, I thought this was going to take several days."

"So, we have to celebrate. Mom, you pick it. What do you want to do?"

"Well, the first thing I want to do is get something to eat before I pass out. I just know my blood sugar's off."

"Okay, but after that?"

"What I really want to do is go see *A Raisin in the Sun* with Denzel Washington!"

"Ooh Mama, that's sounds nice but I think those tickets sold out a long time ago," McKenzie said, taking in the hustle and bustle of Times Square.

"For the price they were charging for those tickets? I don't think so. We still may be in luck. I can check for you–hold on, I need to get this," Jewel said as she pulled her phone from her purse.

"Hey babe, what's going on, the kids okay?"

"Jewel, I have a bit of bad news, Jermane's dad passed away."

"What? We just saw him. How?"

"He had an aneurism." He took a deep breath, "Babe, I know you and Jermane aren't exactly speaking right now, but I think she needs you."

"Right, honey I'm not sure how soon I can get a flight out but I'll try. Call you back soon."

McKenzie and her mom stopped talking once they realized something was wrong.

Jewel dropped her head momentarily. "One of my best friends. She um, just lost her Dad. I'm gonna have to head back."

"Oh, of course," McKenzie said.

Chapter 43 – Airport Shuffle

Jewel rushed into the airport and checked the flights. The next flight back to Houston was at 8:10 p.m. She changed her ticket, checked her bag, and went through security. She sat down at her gate and immediately called Lexi. "Hey Lex, I heard. Have you talked to Jermane?"

"I talked to Rex. She won't talk to anybody right now. He said she's pretty messed up. I think it's the guilt over what happened on Easter, more than anything."

"Oh my goodness, I'm sure she's feeling it pretty tough right about now. All we can do is pray for her."

"That's what we've been doing. Are you going to make it back soon?"

"I'm in the airport now. Shoot!" Jewel looked up at the flight schedule board.

"What's the matter?" Lexi asked.

"A flight delay. It's starting to rain."

"Wow. Well, hang on in there. Call me when you get in."

After another delay, Jewel headed to Chili's to grab a bite to eat. The next flight was scheduled to leave at 9:45 p.m. Once she finally boarded, they were delayed another twenty minutes prior to take off. Once in the air, she couldn't rest. Jewel wasn't afraid to fly but the turbulence was so bad she prayed the whole way. She could have sworn somebody was speaking in tongues a few rows back. The plane was dipping, dropping, and shaking. When she touched down in Houston she could have hit the ground and the pilot.

~~~~~

Jewel was extra grateful that her husband had parked the car and met her inside, which was a huge accomplishment at any Houston airport.

"Baby," he said, standing a few feet away before he grabbed and hugged her. "Missed you. Where are your bags?"

"Your guess is as good as mine," she said, watching the skeletal remains of the bags from her flight. "Looks like they may have lost them." She reported the information, hoping she'd see her bags by the next day. She was so exhausted she didn't care.

"Capri offered to watch the kids until I picked you up."

"Capri? *Capri?*" She blinked in disbelief.

"Yeah, Capri."

Chapter - 44 Grieving Spirit

Jermane remained depressed and hadn't spoken to anyone since her father died. In her eyes the legendary, trailblazing Avery Jacobs was invincible, immortal. Her friends continued to pray individually and collectively for her and her family. She finally pulled herself out of the pit long enough to help with the last part of her father's funeral arrangements. The family was waiting for her to come downstairs to get in the family car.

When she stepped out, she was dressed in a simple white dress, a birdcage veil, white Louboutins and white gloves. "This is a celebration," she said. Once she reached the bottom of the stairs she was stunned to see Albany. Jermane felt a lump in her throat, her stomach constricting in a tight ball. She walked over slowly. She paused and placed her arms around Albany. "I'm very sorry," Jermane whispered.

Albany just nodded as they pulled away. As the two women held a gaze, Jermane could clearly see the hurtful look in

Albany's eye. She held Jewel's hand before she parted. "Better get to the church," she said as she walked off

"Sweetie," Rex grabbed her elbow. "The car is waiting."

"Albany," Jermane took a deep breath. "Ride with us?"

She turned with a faint smile. "I'd like that. And Jermane, just so you know," she paused before they walked out, "I'd already signed a prenup," she swallowed water forming in her eyes, "Weeks ago. I loved him."

~~~~~~

Once they arrived at the church it was filled to capacity with judges, lawyers, members of the NAACP, fraternity, and alumni. It seemed like the entire community was there to send of a trailblazer. Lexi wondered who was running the city. She was proud to see Jermane walk in looking so strong because she was on the program to speak.

When finally at the podium, Jermane stood and looked out at all the people. She froze and nothing came out. Soon Jewel, Lexi, Angel, and Capri walked up to stand around her. She took a deep breath and gave the most moving tribute that brought lots of laughter and tears throughout. She finally closed, "...Anyone who knows my father, remembered he loved his old school music. After my mother passed, he'd play *Say Amen* by Howard Hewitt over and over again. So, as we close his casket for good, it's not goodbye it's until we meet again."

The song played and Jermane could not make it to the chorus before the tears began to fall and her legs buckled. The girls moved in close, wrapped their arms around her and wouldn't let go.

Chapter – 45 – The Simple Life

     Jewel was excited just to spend a simple family night at home. She lay at the head of the bed, flipping through a few magazines. While Chris was glued to the television, Aja, KJ, and Tinka found their spot on the bed. Jewel couldn't help but think how several months ago she thought just sitting around the house was boring, but she cherished the time now. Right before she went to bed they read the Bible and had a little fellowship. Once Jewel quieted herself she said the following prayer.

     God,

     I am so grateful for all my gifts. I know that You assigned me to McKenzie for a reason. Father, I want to finish the work I started. I still want great, well-paying clients but Lord, what's most important to me are family and friends. Aja and KJ are my heart and I could not have asked for a better husband. Forgive me for coveting anything else. If I could ask one thing, I still would like to travel. At someone else's expense. But I know You would never want me to be continuously away from my family. These children and my husband need me. So I'm going to trust You for my future business.

You are the best booking agent in the world. I don't just want success by the world's terms, I want "God success". I can't wait to see the creative way in which You will answer my prayers. Also father, I pray for my friends, you know every need. I'm coming to the realization that Angel may be really leaving. I love all my friends equally and I'm really going to miss her, but You know what You're doing I'm not going to question it. And father, would You please restore Jermane's joy. It's been a month since we've seen her. I know she's struggling. But give her a reason to embrace her life now that her father is with You. In Jesus name I pray, Amen.

Chapter 46 – Your Enemies Will Bless You

Kevin was not looking forward to Monday at the office. He was grateful for a job but some days he wished he could just lie in the bed. He walked in and before he could even sit down, his phone rang. "Kevin Eastland."

"Good morning, Mr. Eastland, so sorry to catch you so early. This is Nancy Walls, from HR. Could you come up to my office as soon as you get settled in? This won't take long."

"Sure thing." Kevin didn't have time to get nervous. He scurried down the hall and took the stairs to the fourth floor and walked directly to the reception area.

"Oh, go right on in, Mr. Eastland," the blond haired young woman said at the front desk.

"That's not a good sign," he thought.

"Hi Mr. Eastland," a heavy set woman with mousy blond hair and very little make-up said as she got up and shook Kevin's hand.

"Okay." He sat in a chair but kept his eyes on hers.

"So, I'm sure you are wondering what this is about. To give you some relief, you haven't done anything wrong. We had an issue in your area, and to be straightforward we are doing some investigation. So whatever we discuss today is to remain confidential."

"Okay, of course." Kevin pressed the tips of his fingers together.

"We had a former employee that alleged she was being sexually harassed. So, she is exhausting the internal process before she can move forward."

"Is this Heather?"

Nancy took a deep breath. "Yes. The only reason I'm being totally honest is because your name came up."

"Whoa, I didn't do anything inappropriate. I'm married and I only tried to help her with her car one day and encourage her," he said calmly.

"We know, Mr. Eastland. The allegations were not against you. They were against Wendell, your boss."

"Wow."

"But he said it was you who was the guilty party. However, Heather cleared your name. Your supervisor is on a leave of absence without pay pending the investigation findings. If he is found to have sexually harassed this employee he will be terminated. We have a zero tolerance policy here."

"Oh, I know about that policy. I took the on-line course."

"Mr. Eastland, you are a hard worker and your reputation is sterling. So keep up the good work. You are valued here." She clasped her hands and made direct eye contact. Her face softened.

Kevin blinked and his eyes grew wide. "Thanks."

"Which brings me to the other reason we called you in here. While Wendell is under investigation you will take his place temporarily. You are now acting Division Manager."

"Oh, okay."

"Think you can handle it?"

"Think so. I've been preparing for whatever God had next, so I guess this is it."

"Great."

Chapter 47 – Barbershop Bond

"Man, that's crazy," Rex said, waiting for the next barber.

"Yeah man," Kevin said, while his barber placed his hand atop his head to keep it still. "Just like that, he was out and I'm in."

"You know that was God," Rex interjected. "Aw, look who's here. The man of the hour," Rex said as Anthony strode in and took a seat.

Anthony grinned, "Go head man with all that."

"Awe snap! That's my dude right there. One of the barbers popped his towel against the chair right after his client eased out. "Need a haircut?" he said after his client paid.

"Yeah, man, but you need to take care of my partner first." He slapped Rex's hand. "Man, I thought you had your personal barber service. Since when do you get your hair cut here?"

"Every now and then I like to roll through and get that barbershop experience. And when your peanut head boy in the chair wants to have some kind of male bonding!" Anthony nodded toward Kevin.

"Don't talk about my head," Kevin yelled from the chair. "You got to admit this is a real man's barbershop. Not like that "barber spa" you go to." He looked at Rex. "What is it … Ladies and Gents salon – oooh fru-fru."

"Funny." Rex grabbed a copy of *Ebony*.

"Now, this place." Kevin looked around. "Has that vintage vibe. Look at these chairs." He hit the side of the chair. "Man and they comfortable. It ain't loud or ghetto. You get a good cut, shave, *and* old school service. Look at these black and white pictures. It's some history up in here. I love my barber man." He said this as his barber poured talcum powder on a large bristle brush and dusted the back of his neck.

"So, Anthony, Meteors going all the way?" One of the other customers asked.

"Man, hope y'all don't choke. We always make it to the ball but lose that glass slipper every time!" Kevin yelled.

Anthony cut his eyes. "Man, that supposed to be funny?" He sucked his teeth and shook his head. "I'm about to renege on these seats I got for y'all."

"Well, I got faith in my man," Rex said as he got in the barber chair.

"So, this Saturday, Capri wants to get everybody together for the next game. Rex, think you can get Jermane out?"

"We'll see," he said as he sat in the chair. "It's been a month since the funeral and she's been holed up in that house ever since. We gotta do something, man. Bout to send her to grief counseling."

"Mo, this is my boy, Rex, so hook him up. Let him know how Edge it Up rolls."

Mo placed his hand on Rex's head. "Aw, this pretty dude right here with all this wavy hair. I got to take my time with this. How you want it?"

"Taper cut, but leave the waves in, dawg," he said as he removed his wire frame glasses.

"I gotchu."

Chapter 48 – Ambush

"C'mon in. She's upstairs," Rex said as he opened the door. Angel, Jewel, Capri, and Lexi walked quietly up the stairs and knocked on Jermane's bedroom door.

Jermane eased off the bed. "Who is it?"

"Okay, girl. Time to get out!" the girls said as they filed in. "Enough is enough."

"I don't believe this." She shook her head. "What do you guys want? I'm fine, and I'm not going anywhere on a Friday night. The last time we had some bright idea like this I ended up at some male strip club. And you all know how that turned out." She smoothed her hair back with her hands and placed her hands on her hips.

"You don't have a choice," Angel barked as she looked around their huge master bedroom. It was three times the size of hers, complete with a glass enclosed reading room and chaise lounge. "Although, if I had this bedroom, I probably would never leave either!"

"You guys aren't going to leave me alone until I go huh?" She looked at their determined faces.

"Nope," they said in unison.

"But can you at least tell me where we're going so I know how to dress?" she said, noticing their casual, but cute, outfits.

"What you have on is fine, trust me."

"I can keep on the jeans, but I need to change my shirt, and put on some make-up," she said, touching her fruit of the loom t-shirt.

Jewel looked at her watch. "You got five minutes."

"Yeah, and I haven't had a kid free night in a minute so let's make it count!" Lexi added.

~~~~

When Jermane came downstairs she gave Rex a kiss.

"Have a good time honey." He smiled as the ladies filed out.

When they got outside, Jermane laughed, "No, you all didn't. A party bus?"

"Desperate means call for desperate measures," Capri said.

"Okay everybody on We're gonna be late. And stay off the

pole. It ain't that kind of party. Jewel, no Instagram photos, and what goes on in the party bus stays on the party bus."

Jewel threw a feathered boa to Jermane. "What the heck." She threw it over her shoulder and relaxed. After about a twenty minute drive with music pumping, they pulled up to the Arena Theatre.

"You guys, really? I didn't even know they still had concerts at the Arena." Jermane laughed. She looked up at the moniker. "70s Old School Jam....The Emotions, The Stylistics, Heatwave, Bloodstone? What the heck did Bloodstone sing? Anybody know?"

They all looked at each other and shrugged. "Okay y'all time to get out," Angel said as the driver let them off at the front. They went through the entrance after having their purses searched and found their seats in the front.

"Girl, it's some soulful people up in here," Jewel said as she saw some of the matching outfits, medallion chains, rubbing thighs, and too tight skirts void of Spanx. "These folk up in here look like they're having major flashbacks. Told you, you could have kept your t-shirt on." she said to Jermane.

The show was supposed to start at 7:30 p.m., but it was 8:00 when the lights dimmed and the announcer came on. Lexi was already yawning and had called home a few times.

Capri turned to Lexi, "Put the phone away and you will not be yawning this early."

When the music from the Emotions *Best of My Love* started, everybody got out their seats, even Jermane. Everyone in the audience sang the song from beginning to end especially the chorus. It was like that with every song. When the Stylistics came on with *You Make me Feel Brand New, You are Everything, Betcha by Golly Wow*, the place went crazy. Old folks were slow-dragging in the aisle. Then Heatwave shut it down with *Always and Forever*. And they finally realized Bloodstone sang *Take to the Sky on a Natural High*.

~~~~

"Omigod! I had so much fun," Jermane all but bounced in her seat. "My dad used to listen to a lot of those songs. It didn't make me sad, it made me smile. Woo!" Her spirit was full of joy and enthusiasm. "Thank you so much for kidnapping me, guys."

"Yeah, I think I had more fun watching the old school fashion than hearing the music," Jewel added as she grabbed the pole in the middle of the bus. "I mean, purple playa-playa suits, lycra, cat suits. It was a visual fashion feast for the eyes."

"Jewel, that's what your kids are gonna say about you when you get that age and go to a Jill Scott concert talking about 'now that was some good music back then'."

"Ha, ha, funny," Jewel said rolling her eyes at Capri. "I'm going to be fine at fifty, sixty until they take me out of here!"

"I loved seeing those older couples dancing," Lexi added. "That's how I want to be with Chris years from now. They were so carefree. Even if for only one night, they didn't care who was watching, they were going to enjoy themselves and get their money's worth!"

"I don't blame them," Angel said. "When you get to a certain point in life all that silly stuff goes out the window. You don't care what people think. You've made it through storms, your children's storms, lay-offs, loss a bunch of stuff."

"I guess you're right," Capri chimed. "Sometimes we worry too much about the small things."

Jermane looked around. "Guys, I don't want to get sentimental but you truly are the best friends in the world. We may work each other's nerves but I thank God for the way he brought us together."

"Awww, group hug, group hug," Jewel commanded and they all filed in.

"Okay y'all I'm hungry, and those hot dogs and cardboard nachos did not do it for me." Angel rubbed her stomach after a while.

"Ooh, how about Mama's Café on Richmond," Lexi's eyes danced with excitement, "Capri, remember we used to go there for cinnamon coffee and study during law school?"

"Awww, sweetie, where have you been?" Jewel looked at Lexi, "They've been closed for a minute."

"Noooo that was a landmark." She shook her head. "I can't believe it. That was a classic. Time is moving."

"No, we're getting old," Angel added.

"Uh, speak for yourself," Jewel said.

Chapter 49 – Greetings from…

Angel's alarm went off and she rolled over. She was supposed to meet Capri for spin class, but knew it wasn't happening. She didn't even have a drink the night before so she was trying to figure out what her problem was. She dialed Capri's cell.

"Hey, girl. I'm not gonna make spin class. I'm exhausted."

"Please girl, I'm not out the bed yet, either. You still coming to the game tonight right? "

"I don't know, girl. I'm trying to recoup from last night. Dang, I can't hang."

Capri laughed. "Girl, you have to come, we got great seats, and I had to do some finagling to get them. We need to support Anthony! These are the playoffs, girl!"

"Okay, okay. I'll be there. Bye." Angel rolled on her back and stared at the ceiling. The soundtrack of the night before was still playing in her head. She sat up and rubbed the bridge of her nose. Despite her exhaustion last night, she had taken the time to twist her hair so it would still look decent. She knew what the disastrous results would have been if she had just let her hair go for the night. She got up and walked in the bathroom. She splashed water in her face. She took a close look in the mirror. "Hmm, no wrinkles." she said as she examined her brown skin. "Jewel's right, I'm still young." She snapped her finger as she noticed her toned arms and taught stomach.

She threw on her sweatshirt, drawstring pants and flip-flops then walked to get her mail. It had been a week since she checked it. She grabbed the bundle made a cup of coffee; well her Keurig spit it out in seconds. She sat at the table, took a deep breath as she sorted through the letters, until she finally got to a small envelope from South Africa. A gradual smile crept across her face. She took a deep breath. *Octavio.*

Dear Angel:

I hope you are well (I already know you're fine – smile). Anyway just wanted to send you a quick note from Capetown. It's so beautiful here I can't describe it. The water, the people, the culture…amazing. I went on a tour yesterday and had a chance to visit Mandela's jail cell. I know it wasn't my struggle but I literally cried. We had worship at a small church and did ministry outreach in one of the communities. I wish you could be here as my words can't do it justice. But I sent you a few pictures just to give you some idea (smile). God is so amazing, I can't explain it. I know you're still waiting on that move of God and I'm praying His complete and perfect will for your life. Please let me know if and when you get the word on that job in D.C. And never forget to answer God's call on your life first and the rest will fall in place. Angel, you were born for this. Sometimes we do what we have to do and I'm keeping you and your mom in my prayers.

Live God's Life Beautifully,

Octavio.

Angel gently placed the letter on the table. She looked at each picture. Octavio was handsome as ever, his olive skin tanned from the sun. He had several shots of the ocean, some of the other missionaries, several from a visit to a game reserve in Kruger Park. He was right it was all beautiful. She held the pictures to her chest, thinking how beautiful God's world was. In that moment, she realized she wanted to see and do more and she wasn't going to hold back. She was going to let God have his way in her life.

She'd never been afraid of much, but she tried to control much of her destiny. If she could have the joy and freedom that Octavio had, she was ready to let God have total freedom in her life. *Have thine own way Lord. Oh, Jesus. I'm so ready.* Just then the Lord gave her a wonderful idea. A way to bless Octavio's ministry and eliminate some much needed baggage before she left for good. *God you're good!*

Chapter 50 – Courtside

"Awww man. I don't know how your boy pulled it off. But I'm loving the courtside action, sweet!" Kevin said as he leaned over to Chris.

"Man, you don't know how much I need this much needed break! I love my work but dealing with the streets of Houston is no joke," Chris said keeping his eye on the game. "Awww naw!" Chris jumped up and placed his hands atop his head. "Ref that's bad call! We see who you working for."

Lexi was seated behind him, and she pulled on his arm. "Babe, c'mon on. So embarrassing."

"Girl let it go. Let the man have a good time," Jewel waved her hand. "Even Rex is into it and you know how calm he is. It's a good game." She looked up at the score. "It's about to be halftime and they're tied. It's a nail biter. Anthony's playing his butt off."

"Yeah, that's my baby!" Capri shouted. Her stomach did flips the whole first half and she was glad everyone came out.

Thankfully, they were able to get a baby sitter for the kids. It was the perfect couples' night out. It was halftime and the floor cleared. Just before the players walked up, the announcer came on. The cheerleaders came out to *Baby, Baby Baby* by TLC and the mascot rolled out a huge baby carriage with a stuffed stork. He had a giant inflatable pacifier.

"Ladies and gentlemen we have breaking news, seems like there's going to be a delivery. One of our player's wives is having a baby." The camera scanned the audience and the Jumbotron lit up, "Congratulations…" A drumroll and the mascot ran over and placed the inflatable pacifier over Anthony's head. He still didn't get it and swatted the mascot away. Finally, he heard his name and saw Capri's face on the screen.

It took him a minute to look up. One of the players tapped him on the shoulder, "Aww, naw man." He placed his hands atop his head. He almost started to cry.

Jewel, Jermane, Lexi and Angel all looked at each other, dumbfounded. They hugged each other and hugged Capri.

Finally, Anthony ran over and reached up to give her a hug as pink and blue balloons fell out of the ceiling. "Okay, honey I gotta go," he said as he ran off the court for halftime.

Everyone looked at Capri in shock. "Yeah, I know. I did that!" She laughed as she brushed her shoulder. "Now, that ladies and gentlemen is how you tell your man you're having his baby!"

Chapter 51 – On & Poppin'

After such a wonderful weekend, Jewel didn't even mind having to head to L.A. She was helping McKenzie host a small Bridal Brunch for her bridesmaids and close friends. She was looking forward to a fun and stress free trip, since most of the details of the wedding were done. She was flying out Thursday to make sure everything was in place for the brunch, and coming back that Sunday. When she was waiting to board she got a call from McKenzie.

"Hey sweetie, I'm about to board, everything okay?"

She burst into tears.

"What's wrong?"

"I don't know … it's Horace. He's tripping. We flew out to Napa and he doesn't like the venue. I described my dress and he said he wanted something sexy. I'm just sick of it." She blew her nose.

"Okay, take a deep breath, McKenzie, it's gonna be fine." *He is a real butthole.* "I promise. Just let me talk to him when I get there. I mean it's your day too and you loved the venue and the dress from the moment you saw them both."

"Yeah I did."

"So let him know how you feel."

"It's not that easy. Jewel."

Jewel rolled her eyes. She had had enough of Mr. Horace and wondered if this wedding should even take place. All this success was going to his head. It was time for McKenzie to stand up for herself or she was going to be an imposter in a marriage and be miserable for life.

"McKenzie, you have an extremely successful business. You don't let your clients or colleagues run over you. Why do you allow Horace to run everything?"

"You're right. I guess because he knew me before all the success and enhancements. He gave me the confidence to start my own business and stand up to my family."

"Fine great, but you had something to work with from the beginning. McKenzie, sweetie, he is not God. You need to start taking ownership of the beautiful and gifted person you are or you will be miserable whether you are single married or have a million dollar business." Jewel was getting furious. "You need to go and read Jeremiah 1:5 like twenty times. You are the gift!"

McKenzie stopped sniffing. "Jewel, you're right. I don't know what I'm afraid of. This is my wedding and my life and I'm no longer giving my power away to anyone." She hung up the phone.

"McKenzie? McKenzie? Oh well." Jewel threw the phone in her purse and picked up her *Essence* magazine and continued to read until it was time to board.

~~~~~

Jewel spent Thursday and Friday assuring all the details of the bridal brunch were in place. She chose the Loft at the Montage of Laguna Beach. Since it was a small affair it was the perfect location. Fresh flowers, a few touches of the wedding colors and placement of her gorgeous engagement photos gave it a person touch. The guests were arriving for the 1:00 p.m. event.

"Mother Myers, how are you. You look absolutely stunning." She kissed her on the cheek. "I thought McKenzie was coming with you?" Jewel said, eyeing her pink sheath dress and statement necklace. Her make-up was soft and youthful.

"No, I spoke with her this morning. She was getting her make-up done. Said she wanted to be by herself to meditate and pray."

"Oh, okay." She greeted two more guests.

"Hello, I'm Jewel Whitaker-Eastland, the Wedding Planner."

"Oh, that's nice." The young woman looked mixed with her hair in a very neat top knot. Her creamy skin popped against her red lips. "Where shall we sit? We're the bridesmaids."

"Oh yes you must be…"

She laughed and looked at Jewel from head to toe, "You obviously are not from around here. Avery Ashton, but if you have to ask, nevermind."

It took every bit of reserve for Jewel not to go H-town on her. Jewel reached way back to her Jack and Jill etiquette training and smiled.

The lady with her lit up. Her blond hair was as shiny and silky as a Pantene commercial. "Hello, I'm Ariane Michaels. The other bridesmaid, a pleasure." She stuck her hand out. "It's your pleasure, I know."

"Well ladies, the hosts will seat you."

Jewel bit her lip as she looked around. It was 1:15 and McKenzie hadn't shown.

"Hi, I'm Natalie, McKenzie's sister."

"Oh, I'm Jewel," she said. Her sister was as gorgeous as McKenzie had stated. She wore the perfect tea length floral dress, with her hair laid, and flawless make up. She was poised and gracious.

"I just had to meet the person that gave my sister her life makeover. Boy was she a train wreck. I used to be embarrassed to claim her. Now, I couldn't be more proud. She's marrying a doctor. A PS, that's ca-ching in my world. I hate her. Every man I've dated cheated. Well, I'm headed to my seat." She tossed her hair, flashed a smile and was about to sashay off.

Jewel was stunned, "Wait, have you spoken with McKenzie?"

"No, I haven't."

Jewel took a deep breath, she was feeling really uneasy.

~~~~~

Jewel walked toward the front of the venue. "Eh-um. Hello Everyone. It appears that McKenzie is running a little late, perhaps some traffic."

Avery had had one too many drinks. "This is such a disaster," she said aloud.

Jewel cut her eyes.

Ariane turned to her, "Why on earth McKenzie picked us as bridesmaids is beyond me. I barely know her." Ariane picked up her clutch. "Look, this is rude and a waste of my time." She stood up and was about to leave when Horace burst through the door.

"Jewel, can I see you for a moment." He said out of breath.

Jewel rushed to the front, past McKenzie's mother, who had a worried look on her face. She followed Jewel.

"What's going on?" McKenzie's mother said in a loud whisper.

"Jewel, the wedding's off." He said it with finality.

"What? How, why?" She queried.

"It's McKenzie, she called it off and it's your fault." His eyes blazing with accusation.

Natalie hit her table, and shot up. "I knew it! Let me call my bestie and collect my money. No way would my sister get married before me!"

Jewel was about to blow. Spasms of fury crossed her face. "I've had enough!"

Ariane and Avery were headed for the door. Jewel backed up and blocked it.

"My baby, I need to find my baby," Mrs. Myer's threw up her hands in a fit of anxiety.

Jewel went and stood on a chair. "Listen up. I have logged countless miles and left my husband and children behind, I've been wedding planner, counselor, travel coordinator, and a darn good actress when called for. Ordinarily I'd say under those circumstances there would be a wedding but," she put her hand on her hip, "you people are horrible and clueless." She turned to Horace. "McKenzie loved you before you became Mr. Plastic Surgeon, Fraternity brother…Mr. Iron Muscle Laguna Beach! She knew you when you were Halitosis Horace! And you need to find a church home or none of this crap is gonna work!"

McKenzie's mother smiled and took her seat.

Jewel continued. "You, Paris Hilton and Nichole Richie...the early years." She pointed at Ariane and Avery, "McKenzie is *waaay* too good for you. She needs to find some bridesmaids that care about her and have the right spirit. You're fired. You can go." She pointed her finger and they marched past with their noses in the air. Jewel snatched the bottle of champagne Ariane had in her hand as she walked by. "Thank you. Now get to steppin!" She stomped her pump. "Natalie, I just met you. But you are jealous and self-centered. This is your one and only sister, and maybe, just maybe if you could take the time to be happy for all her success you'd get somebody to marry you too. Might I suggest a little therapy? Now, I don't know who's gonna pay for all this," Her arms sweeping, "but Montage people please see Horace for the bill. I'm headed back to my hotel.

Horace, I suggest you focus on one thing and one thing alone...finding McKenzie. Because you will not find anyone else with a heart like that. And for your recommended reading may I suggest, *The Five Languages of Love* and the *Bible*. People, love is not a game! It's not a wedding and it is not to be played with." She turned around, and walked out. "I'm outta here!" Just when she stepped out the hotel doorway, she spotted McKenzie standing near the beachfront.

Oh shoot. I thought I was going to be able to make my getaway. Okay God, I got you. McKenzie walked up to Jewel with an almost bare face. She'd washed her hair and let her natural curls loose. She had on a basic t-shirt, ripped jeans and Toms shoes and she looked stunning. "Hey Jewel. I'm sorry. I just couldn't bring myself to fake it another day." She hugged her. "This was a disaster huh?"

"Um, not really. Sometimes things need to fall apart before they get fixed. I'm proud of you." She grabbed her hand and held it. "You could have done all this before we spent all this money and FYI, I cursed everybody out."

McKenzie's eyes grew wide.

"Just kidding, I didn't curse anyone out, but I'm pretty sure Avery and Ariane won't be inviting you to Sunday Brunch anytime soon."

McKenzie looked down then up. "Probably a good thing."

"Look McKenzie, it's time for you to stand up. To everybody. Don't do anything if you have doubts and reservations. Take your time. A wedding is one day, marriage is forever."

She shook her head as she bit her lip.

Jewel took a deep breath, "And don't ever let anyone make you feel inferior or worthless. I mean, we all have moments in our lives when we may doubt ourselves."

"Even you?"

"McKenzie, contrary to legend and popular belief, I'm a bit of a mess. Let me tell you something. I married a man without a degree. He had a beautiful daughter when I met him and a baby mama that used to be on crack. She had a baby and died at the time of her childbirth. Those are the two kids I have now and I love them like they were my own. If I had stuck with the world's idea of happily-ever-after I would have never had my real 'happily-ever-after'. It's messy, fun, crazy and imperfect. But I would not trade it for the world."

"Wow, that sounds like the makings of a reality show."

"Okay, I can say that, you can't…too far." Jewel smiled. "What I'm saying is, you gotta love yourself. If you don't treat yourself well, nobody else will. And just once, go left on somebody!"

McKenzie laughed. "Jewel, seriously. Thank you." She took a deep breath then saw Horace walking toward them.

He walked up to Jewel. "I know I blamed you back there. But I want to say in front of McKenzie that you were right, about everything." He turned to McKenzie. "Sweetie, I owe you a huge apology. I've been very critical and full of myself." He took a deep breath. "How about we start this thing over?" He touched her face softly.

McKenzie wasn't sure how to respond.

He got down on one knee with the sound of the ocean as a backdrop. "McKenzie Myers, I love you just the way you are. You are my best friend and if you would have me, I want to make you my wife."

McKenzie took a few seconds to speak. "Horace, can you please stand up?"

Uh-oh, this can't be good. Jewel watched the scene played out.

McKenzie grabbed his hand and held it. "You already proposed once and I accepted. But I think we have some work to do before we plan a wedding. I love you, but I want to make sure we do this right. There's something really important missing."

"What? The honeymoon? A new house?"

"None of that…" She took a deep breath. "God. If we can't have God then you can't have me."

Chapter 52 – Brunch Full Circle

"Nothing like a familiar place. Breakfast Klub is always on point," Lexi said as her hot plate of chicken and waffles called her name. The space was packed with tables and buzzed with patrons but that made it all the more fun.

"So Jewel, you actually stood in a chair and clowned like that?" Angel asked, amused.

"You know I did!" she yelled.

"If I could have been a fly on the wall," Capri put her hand to her mouth as if she were about to burp. "Oooh Girl, you gonna eat all those pancakes?" She stuck her fork in Angel's plate.

"Girl, go head, you can have all the pancakes you want."

"So have you found out the sex of the baby?" Lexi asked.

"Nope, we want it to be a surprise," she said, not looking up from her plate.

"What is up with you people?" Angel fussed, "I need to know because I can't stand buying yellow and mint baby clothes."

"Well, you're just gonna have to wait."

"So back to the McKenzie tale, are they getting married?" Jermane asked.

"I believe, eventually. They're going to counseling first. But get this ... her real dream wedding? Barefoot at Big Sur." Jewel shook her head as she cut a piece of omelet with her fork and ate it. "All that planning and that's what she wanted all the time. But I think's she gonna wear the Vera Wang. I would too, even if I was going to the J.P."

"Uh Lexi, you gonna eat that last chicken wing? How about that waffle?"

"Dang Capri girl, we get it you are hungry and PREGNANT!"

She paused and rolled her eyes. "But I' m still fine," she said, breaking apart her chicken wing.

"Well, you won't be if you keep eating those troughs of food," Jewel quipped. "Anyway, I'm just glad to be stationary. No more L.A. excursions anytime soon. It was worth it, even if I didn't get a check."

"What, you haven't gotten even a partial fee?" Angel spread butter on her biscuit.   Jewel sighed, "No I don't even care." She sipped on her coffee.

"What?" they all said.

"Well, wait a minute. Somebody better break me off something. But even if they don't pay me, I believe God's gonna find some way to bless my obedience. I believe this was an assignment, maybe a test and I think I passed it with flying colors! Besides, Kevin's now the permanent Division Manager. Think I'm gonna let my man take care of home. Then I can pick and choose my clients for the moment."

"Awww Jewel, that's so wonderful. I'm really proud of you," Jermane said.

"Really?" She smiled. "Thanks."

"Angel, why are you so quiet?" Lexi took a sip of her coffee.

She looked around. "Okay guys. It's finally official. I got the call. The job's mine. I've known for a few days." Suddenly the mood went from festive to bittersweet.

"When are you leaving?" Jermane asked.

She looked around at her girls and sighed, "One month. But I've been packed and ready to go for a while."

Lexi leaned back, "Wow, seems so surreal. What's brunch gonna be like without you?"

Angel shrugged. "It's all a part of God's plan."

"Welp, I guess I need to put my party planning skills to work!" Jewel said, upbeat. "Don't beg and thank me later."

"Uh-ah, Jewel, no party, please. All I want is for you guys to come by my place and hang out for a little while I do some last minute cleaning and final packing. I hate, hate hate goodbyes!"

They all looked at each other. "Party!" They yelled in agreement then laughed.

Angel rolled her eyes. "Okay, just a small one. No props, decorations or fancy-smancy stuff. Just us a little grub and with lots of girlfriend love."

They all grabbed hands while seated at the table, "Agreed."

Chapter 53 – The "Not a Party" Party

Angel was laughing until the tears rolled down her face.
They decided to have just light refreshments, and talk about old
times while Angel finished packing up a few more things. She
decided to keep her place and rent it out. A law student was going
to rent it out in a month or two. "Remember when Lexi tumbled
down those steps at the police station with that afro wig."

"Yeah, Jewel's 70's party. I didn't even realize I'd hurt my
knee because Chris helped me up. Man that was crazy."

They were all sitting on the floor and everyone's emotions
were all over the place.

"Now, how about that dude Kyle you used to date,"
Jermane said to Lexi.

"Girl, please he was like a wolf in sheep's clothing talking
about God sent him as an answered prayer." Lexi rolled her eyes.
"No, remember when my water broke? We should have listened to

your mama Jewel. "On a mission to bust the men at a strip club. Why didn't y'all stop me?"

"We tried!" Capri laughed.

"How about when Jewel got locked up for…" Lexi was about to keep talking until she saw Jewel's face. "Anyway, if it wasn't for Jewel I wouldn't have met Chris. She got up to get some more punch. "Woo, but I'm telling you as much as I love him, marriage is a huge commitment."

"And a lot different than I would ever imagine." Jewel added. "Raising somebody else's children was so not on my vision board."

"Don't get me wrong I would not trade my husband and kid for the world. Chris is so good but I had to realize he's human. Sometimes we have to pay attention because men sure don't spell it out. I've decided to take Little Chris out of that private kindergarten and finding something a little less expensive. I want my man at home and in church with me on Sunday. Not working a double shift."

"I so get that. I truly had to get used to Kevin as the breadwinner. I was so set on having my 'own money' that I was willing to leave my family to get it. But God is so good, I got a

call the other day about possibly coordinating this major event at

Disneyworld. Me, Kevin and the kids would go for free.

McKenzie referred me. So all was not lost! And I did get a check."

"Wow, that's awesome." Angel shook her head. "It took

me awhile but I finally realized how much God rewards our

obedience. We put the limits on ourselves. But He's a big God."

Angel said, "Do you know Octavio is on his third mission's trip?"

"Octavio? Wow. Have you spoken with him, I mean since

you got the offer?" Lexi said fishing.

Angel pressed her lips together before she spoke, "No, but

I've been getting letters from his trips."

"Wow, so inspiring. I mean we work all our lives for what?

We can make our lives as fulfilling as we'd like. Rex and I decided

we're taking a trip. Hey we don't have kids, firms doing well.

Why not? We're thinking Hawaii. Heck, maybe we can start

working on that family." She winked.

"What? Don't try to sneak that in there!" Jewel said. "I

thought you never wanted kids?"

"I didn't say ever. After my dad passed I just thought about his legacy. I talked it over with Rex, and I think he's had a change of heart too."

"Wow, Jermane you'd make an awesome mother!" Lexi hugged her.

"And y'all would make some pretty babies. I think it's almost an obligation for gorgeous people to procreate." Jewel added as she bit her pizza slice." She looked up and they were all staring at her, "What?" She waved her hand, "Nevermind."

"Anyway, back to something more serious. Angel, just curious, so Octavio doesn't know you're leaving tomorrow for D.C.?" Capri pressed.

Angel shrugged, "I sent him a text and let him know I got the job. He has an idea I'm leaving soon." She jumped up and started to clear off some of the paper cups and plates from her counter.

"You sent him a text!" Capri blasted. "All those years together and you sent the man a text. Angel, you're a piece of work."

She shrugged as she folded a paper plate and shoved in in the trash, "I mean, what was I supposed to do?"

"I don't know," Jewel quipped, "but I could think of something better than a text. There's still a part of me that thinks you two belong together. "

"Oh no," Angel started wagging her finger, "It's settled. This train is moving. All doors to the past are closed! Besides, this moment isn't about me and Octavio. It's about me and my girls." She looked around "And I'm really, really going to miss you all."

"Oh boy, don't do that," Lexi said fanning her eyes.

"Seriously, I never really let myself get close to women before you all. This is a cut throat world but you all have been everything to me. When I met you guys I was a hard rock but you turned me into a soft gem. Jewel, you taught me to make life a party. And as much as I resisted and complained, you brought my joy back. Lexi, you taught me to believe in love, you taught me to trust God and to be vulnerable. And who knows … you may get that wedding invite one day. Jermane, you taught me to have grace under pressure. You are the epitome of elegance. You helped me to understand strength isn't always loud or boisterous but often it's quiet and unassuming. Capri, you help me learn how to take chances and to never apologize for my talents and gifts. I'm so proud to call you friend. "

They all sat there doing the very thing they said they wouldn't, balling their eyes out.

Jewel jumped up. "Well, I know one thing I'm gonna do right now. I need to do some research for a fabulous new restaurant for our first... D.C. Brunch!

Chapter 54 – Mission Mail

Octavio had been home for a few weeks and was getting
settled. He'd gone to the post office and had a bundle of mail.
Bills, bills, bills. When he'd gotten to a handwritten envelope he
recognized the writing. He opened the letter and a check in the
amount of $10,000 dollars fell out. He bent down and picked it up.
He stared at it for a few seconds and scratched his head. Then he
read the letter.

Dear Friend,

*By the time you get this letter, I will probably be well on my
way to D.C. I got the official offer but you were still out the
country. You know me. I'm not a woman of many words. I had a
small box of things at my place. I left it with Lexi a week ago. Just
some pictures and personal items. If I had delivered them
personally I probably would have said a bunch of sentimental
things and we would have been right back on this merry-go-round.
So this was best. I sold my car. Please take this money and put it*

towards one of your missions trips. Just consider it a seed – smile.

Anyway, if you should ever find yourself in D.C., well you'll know

what to do. So long for now.

Destiny awaits.

xoxo

Angel

Octavio was stunned. He was so moved by the generous gesture that all sorts of feelings went through him. *Wow, closure.* He paused and somewhere between finality and feelings of loss he decided to pick up the phone and dial, "Lexi, hey…this is Octavio–"

~~~~~

For the first time in her life Angel went through security in record time. She'd called her aunt, who was over the moon that Angel was on the way. Everything seemed to line up. She was actually looking forward to seeing some of her childhood friends and she loved the energy in D.C. She stopped for some coffee, stocked up on magazines and waited for the boarding call. She double checked her phone to make sure it was in airplane mode and took a deep breath. "Welp, to new beginnings. No looking back."

"Flight 3227 non-stop flight to Dulles Airport," the announcer said.

Angel took a deep breath. "This is it." She waited until they finished the pre-board and they finally called her rows.

~~~~~

Octavio had done the craziest thing he'd ever done in his life. He found the cheapest airline ticket he could find and bought it just to get past security. The security line was moving like snails and he finally got through after a full body search. Then he ran down the corridor. He got to Angel's gate and spotted her in the line. She was just about to have her ticket scanned to get on the plan. "Angel!" He yelled as he got close. "Angel!"

She looked around, and seemingly stared directly in Octavio's direction, but continued to walk. Octavio ran to the counter and started rapidly speaking to the airline agent.

"Whoa sir." She put her hands up. "Don't you see all these people behind you?"

"Yes, miss, but I have an emergency." He stuttered out of breath. Oh, forget it. He walked away and frantically dialed Angel's cellphone. "C'mon baby pick up, pick up." She must have turned her ringer off. *God, if she answers, I know this, all this is You.*

The gate finally shut and they were preparing for take-off. He walked over to the window, feeling completely deflated. "What was I thinking?" He thought, unable to bear watching the plane inch away from the gate towards the runway. He turned shoved his hands in his pocket and walked away like a wounded soldier.

When he got to his car, he saw a ticket on his windshield. "Perfect." He snatched the paper and got in his car. He sat in the front seat and let his head fall on the steering wheel. *Guess the silver lining in all this? I didn't get towed.* He lifted his head and was about to start the car but felt his pocket first. He sighed as pulled out the black box and opened it. He grinned as he gazed at the three carat diamond ring he'd purchased over a year ago.

~~~~

When the plane finally taxied toward the runway, Angel raised the shade on her window and peered out. The sky was a delicious abstract of orange, with pink in the distance against a powder blue sky. She took a deep breath as she powered down and relaxed. *God, Houston wasn't all good but when all was said and done, it was all good.*

Once the plane ascended she felt all her weight, cares and concerns release. Closing the Houston chapter of her life had been more difficult, emotional, sacrificial and scary then she'd let on. But she knew deep in her spirit it was God. She turned her body to get as comfortable as the seat allowed. As she drifted to sleep, she faintly smiled, thinking of Lexi, Jewel, Capri and Jermane, the four women that had become more than friends. They were her sisters and she loved them. Then she allowed herself a few seconds to think about the only man that taught her to love–and smiled.

The End

ABOUT THE AUTHOR

Norma L. Jarrett: Author, Blogger, Speaker and Creator of Brunch Lady

Norma L. Jarrett is the author of the novels *Sunday Brunch* (Best Girlfriend Book – *Upscale* Magazine), the *Essence* magazine national book club selection *Sweet Magnolia* and *Essence* bestseller, *The Sunday Brunch Diaries* all published under Broadway books/Randomhouse and *Brunchspiration: A Quotable Devotional, Valentine's Day Again,* and *Love on a Budget.* She is also the creator of Brunch Lady – a lifestyle brand inspired by *Sunday Brunch.* Her work has been featured in *Ebony, Essence, Gospel Today, Jewel, Publisher's Weekly, Rolling Out, and Southern Living, Upscale, USA Today, Walmart promotions* and other media. Norma has also been a featured guest on the Yolanda Adams Morning Show and other media. Among other honors, Ms. Jarrett has received a Certificate of Congressional Recognition for her literary work. She travels the country as a sought after panelist and speaker for events such as the Baltimore Book Festival, Harlem Book Fair, Miami Book Fair and others. Ms. Jarrett is a graduate of North Carolina A & T State University where she was inducted into the Alpha Phi chapter of Alpha Kappa Alpha Sorority, Inc. and Thurgood Marshall School of Law. She is married and resides in Houston, Texas where she attends Lakewood Church. You may learn more about and or/contact her at:

Website: www.normajarrett.net
E-mail: brunchbooks@aol.com
Twitter: jarrettwrites7@twitter.com
Brunchladybooklife.blogspot.com (Blog)